COWBOY HEAT
The Hell Yeah! Series

SABLE HUNTER

Cover by JRA Stevens

Aron McCoy has sworn off women - except for sex. When Libby Fontaine arrives at Aron's Tebow Ranch, she is determined to cram a lifetime of living into a few short months. The doctor has told her that she can't count on her remission from leukemia being a permanent one. Their attraction to one another is instantaneous and overwhelming. But when Aron finds out that Libby is innocent - he backs off. He has nothing to offer a girl who deserves white lace and promises. Then Aron catches Libby pleasuring herself in his stock tank and hears her cry out his name - and the heat is on.

Six brothers. One Dynasty—
TEBOW RANCH
Meet the McCoy brothers and their friends —Texas men who love as hard as they play.
Texas Cowboys and Hot Cajuns – nothing better.

Content Warning
This version of the Hell Yeah! Series contains explicit sexual content. If you'd like a less explicit version please look for the "Sweeter Side" of the Hell Yeah! Series. Same book without the graphic sexual content.

Sable Hunter

Chapter One: Prologue

Hungrily, she kissed a path down his muscular chest, working her way down to his cock. He was magnificently and wonderfully made.

"I need you, Cher. My whole body is on fire for you. Suck it, suck it hard." Tristan tangled the fingers of one hand in her hair; the other kept the door closed, even as the magistrate tried to break through to arrest him.

Danielle was eager to please him. There was nothing she would not do, nothing she would not try – he only had to ask. Lovingly, she molded his strong thighs, gazing up at him with adoration. Increasing the pressure, she used the tip of her tongue to tease the tiny slit at the end of his cock, mimicking the move she hoped this instrument of delight would soon make into her empty, aching pussy.

Libby licked her lips. Oh, yeah! If only she had a guy like Tristan. Giving a man a blowjob seemed like it would be a total turn-on. She squirmed a bit in the hospital bed. What she wouldn't give to know what it was like to make love. Maybe, she would get a cucumber to practice on – just in case. One day, she promised herself, one day she was going to need this skill.

"Come up here, my dear." Tristan pulled her to her feet. "One sweet kiss before we are taken. It's my turn to please you." She thought he was about to kiss her lips, instead he pulled her bodice down gently, cupped her breast and latched his hot, greedy mouth onto her distended, eager nipple.

"Oh, yes, Tris," Danielle massaged his shoulders, kneading the muscles as she threw her head back and moaned. She loved the excitement, the urgency of his passion. The mix of pain and pleasure as he suckled at her swollen breast, using his teeth to tease the distended tip was exquisite. How would she survive without him?

"How are you feeling, Libby?"

"Cheez-n-Crackers!" Startled, Libby threw her romance novel high into the air. It landed square dab on the top of the doctor's bald head. "Sorry, Doc. You scared me!" Libby held her chest, glad that heart failure didn't run in the family.

"Were you reading porn again, Libby?" Doc Mulligan loved to tease Libby Fontaine. She was as cute as she was sweet.

"It's not porn, Doc. It's erotic romance, there's a big difference, you know." She lay still as the physician checked her vital signs.

He was listening to her heart, but it didn't stop him from continuing his bantering. "Oh my, it must have been some good stuff. Your blood pressure is slightly elevated."

Libby blushed and hid her head in the pillow. "It was pretty hot."

"Explain to me the difference between porn and erotica. I need to be informed. Who knows? I might want to pick up a copy of that 'shades of grey' book everyone is talking about." Doc Mulligan managed to keep a completely straight face.

Libby grinned. She liked when the doctor joked around. Due to the disease she had battled for so long, opportunities to socially interact with people were few and far between. Many days, she had been too ill or fatigued to enjoy anyone's company. Now, her blue eyes sparkled and a dimple came out to play, just past the corner of her top lip.

"Not erotica, erotic romance. Huge difference!"

Doc Mulligan laughed. Libby was such a delight. Never a frown, never a down day – no matter how bad the diagnosis. "Excuse me, O ye hedonist extraordinaire."

"Whadjacallme?" Fits of giggles escaped as the doctor made a funny face at her.

"A hedonist, my dear, is a person whose life is devoted to the pursuit of pleasure." All the while, he was making notes on his clipboard.

"All right, sign me up, I think I'd make an outstanding hedonist. Pleasure seems preferable over pain any old day." Even though she smiled, Doc Mulligan knew she was remembering all the trauma she had endured throughout the years. Cancer could be a cruel disease.

"I don't blame you, my dear." Refusing to be negative, he picked back up on their earlier conversation. "So explain it to me. what's the difference between porn and erotic romance?"

"That's easy." She flipped over on her side, so he could listen to her breathing from the back. "Porn is explicit, graphic descriptions of sex. Erotic romance may be a tad explicit, but the girl and boy love each other very much and there's always a happy ending."

"Ah, a happy ending, that's always good." In his profession, he didn't see nearly enough of those.

"Yeah." Libby grew quiet. What she wouldn't give for a happy ending.

"Tell me, Madame Hedonist, do you have any experience being racy?" He knew she didn't, but perhaps he could persuade her to consider it. Not with him, of course. He was a grandpa!

Libby snorted, laughing. "No, of course not. I've just read about it in books, like the one that just accidentally whacked you across the head." Straightening her hospital gown, she scooted around until she presented a prim and proper picture. "You, better than anyone, know that I haven't had the opportunity or the strength for men or sex." She sobered.

Doc Mulligan took her small, soft hand in his. "Let's talk, little one."

"That sounds ominous." Libby stiffened, expecting the worst.

"No, no," he hastened to reassure her. "In fact, I have good news."

Her eyes got big and round with hope. "Good news?"

"Yes, Libby, you're in remission."

A glow of ecstatic happiness flushed her little, heart-shaped face. "Remission? Are you sure?"

"Yes." The old gentleman smiled and patted her hand. "For right now, you're cancer free."

"For right now?" Libby waited for the other shoe to drop.

"Yes." He pulled his spectacles off and met her trusting gaze. "Libby, I won't need to see you again for at least six weeks. We'll do some more tests at that time. We'll be able to tell by your blood count level whether or not the remission is a true one or just a temporary elevation due to the last blood transfusion. For now, I want you to get out of this bed and live life as hard as you can. I want you to travel and date and be as hedonistic and racy as your little heart desires. Doctor's orders."

The possibilities skittering across her mind showed all over her face. "I've been working in the diner, and I have a little money saved. Doc, I could go camping and learn to ride a horse. Maybe, I could even try starting my line of designer handbags. You know if I end up living, I'm going to have to find a way to support myself. I don't want to be a short order cook for the rest of my life. And... and . . ." she blushed sweetly.

"Meet a man and make some of those erotic, romantic fantasies come true, perhaps?" Libby was like a daughter to him. He had been treating her leukemia for a long time.

"I don't know about that," she shyly answered. "I wouldn't even know where to start."

"Sure, you do." He picked up the used, battered book off the floor. "You've been cramming for this exam a long time."

"Reading about something and doing it are two entirely different things." She didn't have much faith in herself. Nevertheless, this was an unexpected reprieve. "It would be fun to try."

"Yes, you need to enjoy yourself, Libby," Doc Mulligan encouraged. "I want you to be happy."

Suddenly, Libby distinctly heard something else in his voice, a wistful tone. "You don't think the remission is a permanent thing do you?" She said the words slowly, dreading to hear his answer.

Determined not to lie to her, he took a deep breath. "With your specific type of cancer, it seldom is. There is only about a twenty percent chance you'll stay in remission longer than a couple of years. However, who knows? Miracles do happen. And we will get a good indication of how it's going when you come back and visit me in a month and a half." Picking up her hand and kissing it, he made her a promise. "We'll pray for a miracle."

Libby squared her shoulders. "Two years is twenty-four months or seven hundred and thirty days. It's not forever." Wiping a happy tear from her eyes, she gave Doc Mulligan a heart-stopping smile. "But, I'll take it."

Chapter Two

"You can do this, Libby." Bess assured her as she scurried around and finished packing the well-worn blue suitcase which appeared to pre-date World War I. "I have complete faith in you. You are a wonderful cook, a good housekeeper, but most importantly, you have a kind heart. I wouldn't abandon my boys to just anyone, you know. I've been taking care of them for six years."

"I'm going to do my dead-level best not to disappoint you, Miss Bess," Libby carried the garment bag and followed the harried housekeeper of the Tebow Ranch to her red minivan. "What's Aron's favorite dessert? What did you tell me?" She wanted to do her best by all of the McCoy brothers, but she especially wanted to please Aron.

"He loves chocolate, anything chocolate. Oh, and early in the morning, he goes crazy over homemade cinnamon rolls and strong coffee. It helps him get going. He's the one you need to pamper. After all, Aron stepped in and took on the responsibility for the entire ranch and all of his brothers when Sebastian and Sue were killed." As she settled herself behind the steering wheel, the older woman caught Libby's hand and pulled her close. "If you need anything, talk to Jacob. He's a rock. Remember, he knows about your condition. If things get too much for you, go to Jacob."

Libby pushed the heavy braid off her shoulder and

13

hugged Bess Morrison. "Jacob is my friend. He has been for a long time. He knows that I don't want the rest of the family to know about the cancer. I feel great, and I'm tired of seeing pity in people's eyes." She grinned and winked at her mother's best friend. "I want to be a normal girl on the make."

"Well, you won't have to look very far for prospects. Five of the McCoys are marrying age – and they're all sexy as sin." The older woman blushed at her own comment. "But Aron has taken himself off the market – or so he says." As she pulled the car door closed, she was rolling down the window. "You could change his mind, if you tried. I know you want to, so don't try and tell me any different. Your Mama knew what was going on. She told me about that bronze you bought all those years ago." Bess looked at Libby Fontaine and saw a precious, beautiful girl who'd never really had a chance to spread her wings and fly.

Libby's face flamed. Was she that transparent? Lord, she would have to be careful. Being the brunt of the McCoy boys' amusement would be highly unpleasant. "Aron McCoy is a legend; he would never be interested in a girl like me. Besides, you know I can't marry anyone. My, my….my future is too uncertain." She looked over her shoulder to see if anyone was around. It would be just her luck to turn around and find her lifetime crush standing right behind her.

"A girl like you?" Bess huffed in reproach. "Any man would be lucky to have a sweetheart like you. Besides, it doesn't have to be about marrying, necessarily. I may be an old fogey, but I'm not that old. Just have a good time." As she backed up, she gave Libby one more directive. "All the boys are special, but take extra special care of my baby, Nathan. You'll probably have to remind him to do his homework every day. Also, watch out for Isaac. He'll pull the wool over

14

your eyes, if you let him. He thinks he's a ladies' man." She put the brakes on, not able to let go of her boys without saying just a few more words. "Jacob is our dreamer, he loves everything about family life and nothing would make him happier than seeing the ranch like it used to be – full of family, fun and tradition. Joseph lives every day like it could be his last. He would walk a high wire, if the circus came to town. Listen to him; sometimes he just needs to talk. Noah tries to come across as all business, but he has feelings just like anyone else." Grabbing Libby's hand, she squeezed it. "And cut Aron some slack if he comes across as unfeeling. He's still recovering from his short, unhappy marriage to that viper Sabrina Jones. He thought he was being 'Mr. Responsibility' by bringing a woman into the house, a surrogate mother for Nathan. Aron was trying to complete the package, do the right thing. But, it backfired on him – big time. Sabrina wasn't wife material, and she certainly wasn't maternal. She sapped all the joy out of Aron, and nearly tore up the family in the process."

Libby hadn't ever heard the whole story, but she couldn't stand the thought of anybody hurting Aron. "Don't worry, Miss Bess. I'll take good care of your boys." She walked beside the van as she waved goodbye to the woman who had given her a great gift. While Bess was off to tend her granddaughter through a difficult pregnancy, Libby would be having the time of her life. Everything she had been dreaming of was at her fingertips: a chance to live on a ranch, an opportunity to learn to ride a horse, acres of beautiful Texas ranchland to explore, and six good-looking men to spoil.

***

Aron McCoy rode alongside his brother. "You know this Libby Fontaine?"

"Yeah, I went to high school with her." Jacob was determined to keep Libby's secret. He intended to be deliberately vague. As long as Libby was able to do her job, her medical condition shouldn't be a factor. After all, it was a temporary gig. Bess was only slated to be gone for three months. "She is an excellent cook. Bess said she's worked at the Kerbey Lane Cafe on Guadalupe in Austin off and on for several years. She was even featured on that cooking show with the guy who has the wild, white hair and wears his sunglasses backwards. You know the one that drives all over the country and features local restaurants on his television show."

"I don't know the show, but I know Kerbey." Aron had played linebacker for the Texas Longhorns and knew the dining choices in Austin like the back of his hand. "They make great pumpkin pancakes."

"I'll ask if she'll whip us up a batch for breakfast one day soon. How's that?" Jacob swung off his horse, an Appaloosa mare, and opened the gate to the stable.

"Sounds good to me." Aron dismounted and led his golden Palomino stallion, Sultan, into his stall. "Jacob, is Libby one of your women?" He knew Jacob had been involved with half the eligible females in the county. At one time, Aron had been as popular with the women as his brothers, but his experience with Sabrina had taught him that loving a woman came with too high a price tag - both financially and emotionally.

"No," Jacob hastened to put that idea to rest. "Libby's a pretty girl, but she and I are just friends." As Jacob removed Abigail's saddle, he glanced over the wall to where his brother was cutting the wire off a couple bales of hay. "She might have her eye on a particular guy already." Libby had no idea Jacob knew of her fascination with his older brother. If she did, she probably would've never agreed to help them out. Jacob longed for Aron to find someone to love - and to his notion, the perfect woman for the job was Libby Fontaine.

***

"Something smells great!" Nathan yelled as he bounded through the mudroom door. Like the rest of his family, Nathan never met a stranger.

"Hi, I'm Nathan." He slid to a stop right in front of Libby. At thirteen, he was already as tall as she was.

Libby laughed at the state of Nathan's boots. "My name's Libby. I see you've been in the barn with the horses." Wrinkling her nose, she pointed at the dirty, smelly footprints he had tracked across the kitchen floor – her freshly mopped kitchen floor. Libby had wasted no time getting into the job. Right now, she was feeling great. Her energy level was practically as high as her level of excitement.

"Whoops. Sorry, Libby." Nathan laughed with her. "Bess would wale the tar outta me for bringing horse poop in to the house on my shoes." He stopped where he was, pulled his boots off and headed to the back porch with them.

"Clean them off while you're back there, don't just chunk them out in the yard." At his laugh, she knew that leaving them dirty had been the original plan. "I won't wale you, but if you'll clean them up and bring me the mop, I'll give you a surprise." Libby knew how to make friends – with brownies. Libby's brownies were a thing of beauty. She took a couple of plain boxes of brownie mix, substituted cream for water, butter for oil, added extra chocolate syrup, a ton of chocolate chips, and a couple of teaspoons of instant coffee, and voila, she had a masterpiece. She called them her orgasmic brownies, not that she had a whole lot of experiences with orgasms, but she lived in hope.

With a sugary incentive like brownies, it didn't take Nathan long to get the horse manure off his shoes and return with the wet mop. "Bess said you are really nice and that I would love the food you'll fix for us." He hung his backpack on the back of one of the kitchen chairs and plopped himself down to wait for his treat.

"Let me clean this up and I'll cut you a man-size brownie," she promised him. Nathan was already a handsome young man. She could see the family resemblance strong in his features. All of the McCoy boys were incredibly good-looking – Aron especially. She was nervous about seeing him for the first time, not that he would know her from Adam. Libby had existed on the periphery of Aron McCoy's world. She had been in junior high when he finished high school, but she had never missed one of his football games. The leukemia had struck her the next year, but she had still kept up with him when he had played college ball and rode the rodeo circuit. Finishing with the touch-up, Libby returned the mop to the back porch. "There, we've got that spic and span again." Washing her hands in the sink, she proceeded to serve Nathan a huge slab of chocolate confection and a tall glass of milk.

"Thanks, Libby." Nathan's eyes grew big with pleasure. He took a huge bite and sighed blissfully. "This is better than anything Bess ever fixed." High praise, indeed.

"I appreciate you saying that sweetie, but don't tell Bess, you'd hurt her feelings. She loves you very much." Libby sat down beside him and began the makings for a huge green salad.

Nathan studied her while she worked. "You sure

18

are pretty, Libby." Even though he was barely a teenager, the compliment made her blush. She was not used to flattery. In fact, no male had ever told her she was pretty before.

"I don't know if I'm pretty, but it's nice of you to say so." Libby grinned at him. "Kind words will not get you out of your homework, however."

"Aw, Libby." She was relieved that they seemed to be getting off on the right foot. Taking care of Nathan was one part of the job that she had been worried about. Cooking and cleaning would be a breeze. The only other concern she had was acting normal around Aron. It would be awful if he discovered that she fancied him.

"What time's supper?" Nathan asked between bites. Typical boy, he couldn't finish one meal before worrying about the next one.

Libby glanced at the clock on the wall. "It's four o'clock. I'll have it on the table by six. How does that sound?"

He nodded his approval of her timetable.

"Why don't you do your homework in here with me? I'll try and help you, if you need it." She hoped his lessons wouldn't be over her head. Libby had missed a great deal of school between chemotherapy and blood marrow transplants. Still, she had managed to graduate from high school and had even taken a few courses at the Austin Community College, courtesy of The Rockwell Foundation. Libby's earnings at the diner barely covered her rent. Her medical bills were either all government gratis or part of the hospital's teaching program. The Rockwell Foundation specialized in giving a helping hand to people trying to build a life for themselves while they lived with cancer.

Nathan hung his head. All of a sudden he looked extremely uncomfortable. Libby didn't push, if he had something to tell her, he would. "I have trouble with my school work sometimes," he confessed softly.

Sitting down beside him, she got her own brownie to munch on. "That sounds pretty normal. I've had trouble with some of my subjects, too." And that was no lie. Just as soon as she would catch up, another flare-up of leukemia would set her back in her school work.

"Yeah, but I was born with something they call dyslexia. I can read pretty good, if I take my time and concentrate, but its writing papers that eats my lunch. I have a paper to write, and I dread it because I have a hard time spelling and using words." He looked so miserable that she gave him another brownie.

"I'll tell you what...I met this girl a few years ago that has the same condition you have. She's a junior in college now, and writes papers all the time. I know she uses some type of special program on her computer that's made just for people with dyslexia. I'll call her and check it out. How does that sound?"

"Thanks, Libby." Nathan smiled at her as he drained the last of the milk from his glass with a slurp. "I'll take any help I can get." Libby laughed. The youngest McCoy was going to be easy to love.

***

"Are you banned from the pool hall?" Joseph asked Isaac as he stepped up on the wide front porch.

Isaac was the bad-boy of the family. Each of them had dealt with their parent's death in different ways. Joseph had turned into a daredevil and Isaac spent most of his time acting out. It seemed that he thought the more hell he raised, the less pain he would feel. He had spent two nights in jail and that was just within the past three months. "Not yet, Shorty's threatening me, though."

"Why did you see the need to rearrange that

stranger's face?" Joseph eased down into the swing. None of them had wanted their mother's outdoor furniture removed, but as the McCoy brothers had matured and filled out, the furniture got smaller and smaller.

"He was full of shit, that's why." Isaac was unrepentant. He lowered his voice, just in case Aron was nearby. Without a doubt, he was still in the doghouse over last night's pool hall incident. "How was I to know that cocky little Yankee would be so sensitive? I didn't really intend to insult the out-of-towner, but I didn't believe for a minute that man had played in the finals at Vegas. I could have let that lie pass, but when the skinny little weasel claimed to have beat Minnesota Fats, I couldn't keep my mouth shut." Isaac laughed, remembering. "I told him the only way he could have won that match would have been if Fats was blind drunk and had one arm tied behind his back. The idiot popped me right upside the mouth. I guess I should have kept my trap shut, or lowered my voice. But hell, I'm a McCoy; I don't have the ability to whisper. One thing led to another, but the end result was the best damn bar fight I've had in at least – well, three weeks."

Isaac was so busy telling his story that he didn't see Aron standing right behind him. "I guess you'll be working off the damages."

Shit! "Where did you come from?"

"I walked up right behind you, Badass." Aron stepped around his brother. "Wash up, supper should be on the table." He stepped into the Tebow ranch house. It would always be his mama's home. Looking around, he appreciated the workmanship on the massive log structure. His daddy had built it with his own two hands, with his and Jacob's help. The interior had been lovingly designed and decorated by the most gracious lady that ever walked the hills of central Texas. Aron would always miss his mother. Sabrina sure hadn't made any effort to put her stamp on the place. All she had wanted to do was spend McCoy money like it was going out of style – and flirt with his brother Jacob. To give the gentle giant credit, Jacob had been oblivious to most of it. And the morning he had caught them in bed together, Jacob had slept through most of the whipping he had tried to give him. Aron had dragged him out of the bed before he realized that Jacob had not even known Sabrina had crawled under his covers. She was just trying to start some shit, and she had succeeded. Aron had moved her off Tebow land that very afternoon.

The divorce had taken three months to finalize. Sabrina still carried a grudge. For some unknown reason she had expected a hefty divorce settlement. After all, the McCoys were well-off. But, Aron's lawyers had seen to it that she walked away with almost nothing. That had been four years ago. Four years without a woman. Four years without sex – unless you counted the times he let himself get overly friendly with his right hand. Yanking his own dick was no substitute for making love. Sometimes he missed pussy so bad he ached, but he certainly didn't miss Sabrina. Now, he was determined not to bed a woman unless it was on his own terms – no rings, no strings, and no promises. It was hard to find a woman who would agree with his terms, especially in this neck of the woods.

Everybody knew the McCoys, and they knew what the family possessed. Women tended to want a secure future, and Aron McCoy had security written all over him. But, he was determined to stay foot-loose and fancy free. Hell, before it was over, he'd probably have to use that damn pocket-pussy Isaac had bought him for a joke. Shit, no! The day he poked his hungry dick inside of that cold, unfeeling plastic was the day he would know it was time to hang up his hoe.

***

He would be walking into the dining room at any moment. Steady. Steady. Libby cautioned herself to remain calm. The meal had turned out better than she'd anticipated. She had decided to prepare one of her specialties: rich lasagna made with Italian sausage, flavorful buffalo mozzarella and a homemade marinara sauce that would knock your socks off. It tasted as good as it smelled. She had sampled a little corner of the finished, gargantuan casserole. Libby loved to cook, but feeding six large males would be a challenge. She would have to tweak all of her recipes to make sure she made enough for everybody to have seconds, as well as leftovers for midnight snacks.

As each brother came in, she had met him with a smile and a huge glass of sweet iced tea, the elixir of choice in the south. Of course, she knew Jacob. He had been President of the Junior Service Club as a teenager and he had single-handedly taken on her cause. Several times, he had headed up fundraisers and benefits to raise money for her treatments and untold medical bills. That was Jacob, a gorgeous hunk with a heart of gold. He was always involved in the community. Libby knew he coached a little league team and served on the disaster relief committee at the community center.

The rest of the boys she knew by sight only. None of them had ever been formally introduced to her. Jacob did the honors. They didn't have any memory of her at all. Libby wasn't surprised, for most of her life she had felt invisible. There had been no dates, no proms, no slumber parties or gossip sessions.

Cancer tended to make you an island. The only attention she had been used to receiving was during uncomfortable appearances at the charitable events held in her honor, or while enduring the poking and prodding of a bevy of medical students in a teaching hospital. When you didn't have adequate insurance, the teaching hospital was where they usually sent you. Putting those sad thoughts out of her head, she focused on the rest of the McCoy family.

Joseph was a doll, Libby noticed. He was very comfortable in his own skin, exuding a confidence that is rarely seen in a man under thirty. "Miss Libby, it's a pleasure." She felt her cheeks warm as he kissed her hand. Jacob had told her his brother was an extreme sports nut – a very successful one. He rock-climbed, raced dirt bikes, rode bulls and busted broncs. Libby knew that whatever Joseph did, it suited him well. His body was in tip-top condition.

Isaac had walked in and picked her up, swung her around and then introduced himself. She had dissolved in a bout of giggles at his: "Finally! A woman in the kitchen that I can intimidate." He had set her down and formally shook her hand. "Libby, don't believe half of what you hear about me. I'm not as bad as they say I am."

"He's worse," Noah interjected as he accepted his icy beverage. "Isaac is our resident badass." He had held Libby's hand and turned her around slowly, as if she was standing on a lazy-susan. "Goodness, you are a little doll. If I wasn't already in love with a tall willowy blonde…" he ended wistfully.

"Harper Summers doesn't know you're alive." Isaac quipped. Something that could have been hurt passed over Noah's features. Jacob had told her that Noah was the practical one of the family. He had a good financial head on his shoulders; Tebow Properties had

24

flourished under his care. While Aron managed the trust fund that their parents had left, Noah managed the day-to-day finances for the ranch. He was a heady combination - a Greek God physique, a handsome face and a beautiful mind. Libby decided she was in beefcake heaven.

Nathan had helped her set the table. She was going to fall for Nathan, hard. He was thirteen, and although she was too young to be his mother, he rattled every maternal bone in her body. Libby knew that the likelihood of her ever having children was slim to none. So the chance to spoil this young man was going to be pure pleasure.

The McCoy brothers surrounded her, teasing and playing, making her laugh at their jokes and smile at their antics. They were doing their dead level best to make her feel at home. From out of nowhere, a chill ran up her spine and her toes began to tingle. What in the world?

Then she felt the heat.

Aron. It had to be.

Refusing to look around, lest she betray her fascination, Libby pretended immense interest in what Jacob was saying, even though she wasn't comprehending a word.

Aron McCoy walked into the dining room and his cock went stiff as a board. When he saw the dainty little doll standing there in the midst of his rambunctious family, he felt like someone had whacked him upside the head with a 2 x 4. As his gaze hungrily moved up and down her exquisite curves, his blood pressure shot up like a rocket and a sudden burst of heat rushed through his body.

Lord Have Mercy!

Aron almost forgot where he was. He had been

lured by the incredible smell of Italian food and the warm, enticing scent of garlic bread. His stomach was doing cartwheels, begging to be introduced to the dishes responsible for wafting those delicious aromas. When he stepped into the dining room, however, all thoughts of food went sailing out the window.

Lord Have Mercy!

She was breathtaking.

He didn't know where to look first, or where to look longest. Tight jeans encased a sweet, heart-shaped little butt that made him want to bare his teeth. Her legs were long and all he could think about was what they would feel like clasped around his hips. A form-fitting, red T-shirt proclaimed that she was "Raw Honey – Sweet as Sugar, Twice as Addictive". The implications of those words practically had him bowing at her feet. He bet her cream would taste like raw, wild honey. His fingers itched to see if he could make them meet around that trim little waist. When his eyes roved northward, tears almost came to his eyes. She bounced a little bounce in response to something funny that Jacob had said, and when she did, he wanted to step forward and catch those sweet little tits before she hurt herself. Maybe, he ought to change his job description – he could go from being a simple cowpoke to a full-time, full-service breast support man. By their jiggle and wave, there was no doubt in his mind that those tits were real and in dire need of about an hour of attention from his hands and tongue.

Realizing he was about to embarrass himself, he took off his Stetson and held it below his belt buckle, effectively hiding her unexpected and tremendous impact on his libido. His smooth move did not go unnoticed by Noah, who smirked from across the room. Casually, Aron shot him the finger. Asshole. He couldn't remember the last time a woman had affected

26

him this way, if ever. Watching his brothers surround the tempting little morsel, Aron opted to utilize a tactic which had come in handy when the McCoy's would be out carousing pre-Sabrina. They had tried to avoid stepping on one another's toes, romantically speaking. Whenever one would see a little filly who caught his eye, he would look at her and simply say one word that would alert the others that she had been claimed and was strictly off-limits to the rest of the McCoys. Stepping closer to the table, he loudly proclaimed, "Tag!"

As soon as the word had left Aron's mouth, the younger men looked up at him in surprise. Isaac bit back a snort, and Jacob simply said, "Thank God." Their brother had finally decided to come out of hiding.

Libby wondered at the word Aron shouted. Was this some type of fire drill or a weird game they played? She could feel him looking at her, 'God give me strength', she prayed.

Libby, as of yet, had not turned to face him fully. And he had to see her – now. "Turn around, Baby. Let me see your face." Confused, Libby did as he requested. Slowly. Uncertainty made her hesitate, but when she had made a complete 180, she heard him catch his breath and she raised her eyes.

Aron.

There was no way she was going to hide the joy that she felt, so she didn't try.

Her smile lit up his world. His body began to instantly heat as if it had been graced by the warmth of the rising sun. Aron tried to move forward, but he was frozen, immobilized, entranced. Muscles that he hadn't used in a while began to loosen, and before he knew it, Aron McCoy was smiling. My Lord, the woman had the cutest, sweetest face he had ever laid eyes on. All he could focus on were her pink, kissable lips. They were trembling ever so slightly. Aron felt the world tilt just a fraction, he wanted to follow that irresistible pull and enjoy the silky softness of that delectable mouth. He heard her let out a soft, sweet sigh.

Memorizing her features, he let his eyes slide over the smooth curve of her cheek, the endearing turned up nose and cheekbones that begged to be traced with his tongue. When he met her gaze, Aron was surprised by the beautiful color of her eyes. They were huge, a deep dark violet, surrounded by smudgy dark lashes that made them look like amethysts nestled in velvet.

Knowing she expected him to say something, he tried to get his brain to engage with his mouth. All he could manage was "Where did you come from?" As if his words released the brakes on his feet, he found himself walking up to her as bold as could be. There was no way he could hold himself back. He had to be as close to her as possible. She stood her ground, bless her heart.

Time slowed down, and she lost herself in the wonder of his nearness. For years, she had dreamed of the day when she would be this close to Aron. He was a big man. Shoulders as wide as a John Deere tractor were encased in a crisp, white western shirt – the kind with the silver snaps. As she looked at him, she couldn't help but think how it would feel to reach right up, grab that shirt right under the collar, and just jerk it open. Those snaps would come in handy if one wanted to get him naked in a hurry. She bet his chest was magnificent, ripped and sculpted. He would look just the way those heroes were described in the romance novels she loved to read. Would his skin be smooth or would he be sexily furred? Damn, it would be fun to find out. 'Look up, Libby, look up' she thought to herself. She knew her eyes were hung up just north of his belt buckle. Gravity and lust were pulling them south. With a jerk, she looked up and when their eyes clashed, she felt it clear down to her pink parts. God, he was potent.

If she didn't touch him, she would die. She took a deep breath. 'All right,' she thought, 'let's go for casual and friendly.' "Aron, it's good to meet you. Thanks for letting me fill in for Bess. I promise to work hard, and I will take good care of you…I promise." Geez, how lame could you get. Oh, well. She offered him her hand.

'Hell yeah! You'll take care of me, no doubt about that.' He'd lay awake tonight imagining the ways she could take care of him. Aron forgot about the five pairs of eyes which were watching them in rapt attention. He just had to touch. A handshake was much too mundane to satisfy this particular need. His hand met hers. First touching the tips of her fingers with his own, he slid the palm of his hand up hers, before finding the pulse at her wrist with his forefinger. When he could feel the beat of life that flowed through her veins, he caressed that spot, memorizing the rhythm. A sweet little gasp escaped her lips and she shivered. Damn! Her whole body trembled, as if in the first throes of orgasm. Aron closed his eyes, realizing this was one woman who would be capable of turning him inside out.

Libby leaned toward him; her breasts almost touched his chest - almost. She could feel her nipples swell in greeting. It was as if there was an irresistible, gravitational pull between her body and his. Shyly, she looked up at him. His eyes were the color of a dark blue lapis. If she were more schooled in the ways of men, she might have thought she read desire in those lazuli eyes. Not possible. This was Aron. And she was just…just Libby.

"Our supper is getting cold. Do you think you two could tear yourself away from each other long enough for us to eat?" Isaac always said just what he thought.

At the break of the incredible tension in the room, the boys began taking their chairs.

"Shut-up, Isaac. Mind your manners." Aron didn't turn loose of Libby's hand; instead, he turned it over in his own and led her by it to the dinner table. Waving at Jacob to move out of the way, he held the vacated chair out for Libby to sit in. It was the chair to the right of his. Jacob had to move to the other side of the table. He didn't seem to mind.

"I need to serve the food," Libby began. Aron pointed to the stove and then to Joseph, who stood and proceeded to pass the lasagna and the garlic bread to Noah, who started it down the table for the family to each dish a portion of the delectable food onto their plate. The boys were bamboozled, since they had never witnessed their older brother acting this way. He was eating Libby up with his eyes, as if she was a lioness in heat and he was the predatory head of the pride, the only male allowed to mate.

Looking around at the puzzled expressions, he ordered. "Eat." They instantly obeyed.

Turning his attention to Libby, he realized he was still holding her hand. It was his eating hand, so he was eventually going to have to turn it loose. Reluctantly, he did so. Now, it was time to get down to business. "Libby, I'm Aron, the eldest of these useless rascals."

His eyes crinkled at the corners when he smiled. Libby wanted to reach out and soothe the sexy little wrinkles. He had a heavy five o' clock shadow that she would give a thousand dollars to feel rasp across her breasts. Whew! It was a good thing she didn't have a thousand dollars or she would be propositioning him right here at the supper table. Finding her voice, she managed to answer. "I know who you are, Aron. When you played ball for Kerrville, I rarely missed a game," she confessed shyly.

30

"Why don't I remember you?" He visually caressed every nuance of her face. She was so exquisite that he wanted to have her for supper, rather than the lasagna.

Libby racked her brain for a way to answer his question and not give away too much of the sad truth. Leukemia had come calling, and effectively took her out of all social circles. She didn't have to answer. Thankfully, Jacob came to the rescue. "You were the alpha male, Aron. The rest of us mortals merely existed on the outskirts of your orbit. Libby's twenty-five. She would have been in junior high when you were reigning supreme on the football field and behind the lockers."

"I hate I overlooked you, I bet you were as cute as a button." He never even looked over at Jacob. Accepting the passed around dishes from Joseph, who sat at his left, he filled his plate with lasagna, and then he served Libby's plate. "There you go, Sweetie. Eat up." Apparently, it was important to Aron that everybody eat their fill. More than likely, this was his way of ensuring their well-being.

"Thanks, I hope you like the food." Libby's appetite was completely gone, or rather, it had changed its focus. Now, her appetite was for one scrumptious cowboy who was setting her heart to racing a mile a minute and making her sweat in places that didn't bear thinking about. Nathan, who sat to her right, elbowed her. She jumped and faced him. "Hey! What was that for?"

"This is the best food I've ever put in my mouth, Libby. I want you to stay with us forever."

Instead of making her feel complimented, the words served to sober her up. Forever. She didn't have forever. She had two years, at the most. Maybe. Two years to live a lifetime, and Tebow ranch was where she would begin.

"You had better never let Bess hear you say that, Nathan." Noah shook his fork at his younger brother.

"How long will you be with us, Libby?" Joseph reached for the butter, even though the garlic bread already dripped with the creamy condiment.

"I guess it all depends on how Bess's granddaughter gets along. Maybe I'll be here three months, six at the most. That is…if you're pleased with my performance." At her words, Aron groaned audibly.

All eyes turned to him, and he had the good grace to look slightly chastened. The innocent words which had come from her tempting mouth had gone straight to his dick. He definitely wanted to be on the receiving end of one of her performances, and by God, he needed to perform in the worst way. "I'm sure we'll get along just fine." There. That sounded like he was halfway sane.

"Have you ever lived on a ranch before, Libby?" Noah asked between bites.

"No, but it's always been a dream of mine. While I'm here, in my spare time, I would like to experience everything about ranch life. I want to learn to ride a horse, rope a calf. I'd even like to help with the harder work like branding." This confession made the boys all talk at once. All of them were volunteering to teach her their specialty.

"Hey!" Aron quelled the racket. When all was quiet, he simply stated. "Whatever Libby wants to learn, I'll be the one teaching her." At Libby's confused look, he tapped her on the end of the nose and smiled another one of those ten thousand watt scorchers.

Effectively, he changed the subject. He didn't know how he felt about the other boys spending time with Libby. She might not be Sabrina, but he didn't want another woman coming in between him and his family. Besides, he wanted Libby all to himself. "How do you know Bess?" There, that seemed like a safe enough
32

topic.

"She and my Mom were friends for years. They went to school together. Mom's gone now, my Dad, too."

"So, you're all alone. Sorry, Honey." Aron looked serious for a moment, and then he continued eating.

Libby went back to her food, then something wild started happening under the table. Several times, she felt his knee bump hers, linger, and then rub gently. Once could have been an accident, but three times? It had to be intentional. The implications had Libby's head spinning. This attention from Aron was more than she had ever dreamed possible.

"I'm grateful to Bess for bringing you to me." Aron's softly whispered words flowed straight to her breasts. Instantly, her skin began to tingle and grow warm and her nipples swelled and hardened. Before she realized it, they were eagerly protruding, and the thin little T-shirt was an insufficient barrier from prying eyes.

Seeing the effect his words had on her, Aron instantly excused himself and in a moment returned with one of his shirts from the laundry room. Draping it over her shoulders, he whispered. "Slip this on." He winked at her as she flushed as much from arousal as embarrassment. "I'll take care of you."

It had gotten quiet at the table, "What?" Aron challenged. "Libby was cold."

At last, the meal was over. Everyone was very appreciative of the lasagna, the salad, the garlic bread and the blackberry cobbler she had whipped up from the fresh berries in the crisper. Bess had plenty of food laid back for her to use, she wouldn't have to do much grocery shopping for a while. When Nathan was through, he stopped at her chair and kissed her cheek,

"Thanks for everything, Libby. Especially the help with the homework. And the brownie," he grinned.

"Where are the brownies?" Isaac zeroed in on the mention of chocolate.

"That huge cookie jar by the rotisserie is full. Help yourselves."

"Don't eat them all," Aron cautioned.

Before she thought, Libby put her hand on his arm, and whispered, "Don't worry, Aron. I saved half the batch back for you. They're in your office in a plastic tub. Bess told me that chocolate was your weakness."

Chocolate wasn't his only weakness, that fact was quickly becoming apparent. Aron was touched. He didn't know what he enjoyed more, the news of the chocolate treats hidden back just for him or the light touch of her hand on his skin." The touch. Definitely the touch, he decided.

Jacob herded out those who wanted to linger around Libby. He wanted to give his brother room to work. Things were heating up much faster than he had ever hoped they might. Aron had been so hurt by his ex-wife. She had moved into Tebow and proceeded to make them all miserable, especially Aron. Sabrina had spent Aron's money as if she was pouring water through a sieve. Then, there was the 'incident', when he had been a pawn in Sabrina's ploy to destroy Aron. And it had almost worked. But, Libby had the power to change everything. Libby could be an answer to his prayers.

This was the first time he had seen Aron show any signs of life around a woman in years. Jacob was fascinated, because Aron's desire for Libby had hit harder and faster than anyone would have ever believed. With a grin on his face, he left them to it.

"You don't have to help me; I'll have this straightened up in a jiffy." Libby worked automatically and quickly, flushed with heightened awareness. God,

Aron made her so nervous. It was wise to keep her hands occupied, she had never been so tempted to throw caution to the wind and aggressively touch a man in her life. This side of her was a surprise. Oh, she knew she liked to read about sex, but she didn't know her blood would run so hot. Only the fear of rejection made her keep her hands to herself.

"The quicker we're finished, the quicker I can take you in my arms." Shocked, Libby stopped and simply looked at him. Could he read her mind? Was he serious? Dared she hope? This was exactly what she had yearned for. Doc Mulligan had said this was her chance, the time to do whatever she longed to do, and experiencing love – or sex – was at the top of her list. To be able to love Aron would be the fulfillment of her dearest dream. "You can shut your mouth, Baby. You're gaping." Laughing, he took the dishrag from her hand and proceeded to wipe down the table. Pulling herself together, she washed up the last of the pots and started the dishwasher to do the rest. Aron made her hyper-sensitive, primarily because she was aware of every movement of his body, every accidental touch, every breath he expelled. Finally, they were through. Libby spread the washcloth over the central divider of the sink, and turned to see what Aron was doing.

He was right there. Lord, in heaven. He was right in front of her. Brazenly, he took one half-step forward and they were suddenly touching all the way from chest to hip. A surprised gasp of delight escaped her lips and she felt a little faint.

Before she knew what was happening, Aron had framed her face with his big, warm hands. She looked up at him. God, he was so tall and broad. The thought passed through Libby's mind that she could settle herself against him, and with his arms wrapped around her, nothing would ever hurt her again. Aron could keep all her ghosts at bay. It seemed that he could even keep the specter of leukemia from ever touching her again.

Aron was in lust-shock, pure lust-shock. His big hands cupped her soft, little face. Out of nowhere, she turned her head and kissed his hand, her sweet gesture almost brought him to his knees. His stiff rod jumped in his drawers. While she had been working around the kitchen, he had been enjoying himself, studying every inch of her delectable body. Aron couldn't believe it. Libby was absolutely perfect. Perfect breasts. Perfect hips. Perfect legs. Perfect for him.

"Libby, may I kiss you?"

He moved his thumbs over the pretty pink blush on her cheeks, sending a ripple of excitement through her.

"Don't say no. I think I'll die if I don't get a taste of you."

Goosebumps rose over every square section of her body. Aron wanted to kiss her! "Please," was all she could manage to say. When he lowered his head to capture her lips, he blocked out all the light. She welcomed the darkness; it was momentous, like the total eclipse of the sun. God in heaven! Aron didn't rush, he relished. Beginning with the softest kiss imaginable, he let their lips introduce themselves, one to the other. Light little caresses, delicate little forays with his tongue that made Libby want to reach out and grab it with her teeth. She made a tiny little grunt of frustration that made Aron laugh with delight. "You are too cute."

She couldn't resist, her hands wouldn't be still. She placed them on his biceps and explored the intriguing bulges. "Hmmm," she groaned as she felt them tighten under her exploration. Aron still hadn't kissed her fully, he nibbled on her top lip and licked at the corners of her mouth, all torture designed to heat her up into a tizzy. Standing on tiptoe, she tried to take over the kiss.

Waiting a lifetime for something made one highly impatient.

Without warning, Aron picked her up and sat her bottom down on the kitchen counter. This put their heads on the same level, and he didn't have to bend over. With one hand, he swept her knees apart and stepped in-between them. Reaching behind her, he clasped her hips and pulled her forward. "Wrap your legs around my waist. I need to feel your heat."

Shaking with desire, she complied with his wishes, but she let hers be known also. "Kiss me right, Aron. Full on the lips. I'm so hungry for you." At her frank request, he stepped back to take it all in. She was delightful!

"You little minx." He reached over and bit her where the soft skin of her neck met her collarbone. "I'm getting to it, don't be so impatient. I've waited a lifetime for someone like you, so let me play."

Despite his instructions to be patient, she just couldn't. Feeling brave, she wrapped her arms around his neck and pulled him forward. He grunted with approval. "Hell, yeah." Then, he gave her what she wanted. Finally. Hands sliding to the base of her neck and tightening in her hair, he fitted his mouth over hers; he sucked on her lips, taking in all of her sweetness. Her little tongue darted out and met his full on. They twirled and swirled, tasting and nipping, devouring one another in a blissful kiss. Thank God for her erotic romances, she knew exactly what to do. Hooking her feet behind his knees, she pressed herself to him. He pulled away from her, resting his head on her shoulder, breathing harshly. "My God, Libby. You're like a little stick of dynamite."

Holding him tightly, she kissed his neck, taking little bites, then soothing them with her tongue. "Is that bad?" His heart was racing, but then so was hers. When

Sable Hunter

he wasn't able to answer, she finished her thought. "And to think, this is my very first kiss."

It took a moment, but her words finally sunk in to Aron's thick skull. Fighting reality, denying what he had heard, Aron let his lips brush over her neck, up the smooth line of her jaw, and around to the tender place under her ear. "What did you say?" Surely, he had heard wrong.

Libby hadn't stopped her sensual onslaught. She was about to give her first hickey – ever. He tasted so good. She sucked on his neck like she was auditioning for a vampire movie. She wanted more. Reluctantly, she stopped long enough to answer him. "You're my first kiss. My life so far hasn't been exactly normal. I've been sort of isolated and out of circulation, family problems..." she offered against his skin.

With one last sweet kiss, Aron pushed back from her until only their hands were touching. "Baby, are you telling me that you're a virgin?"

He didn't look happy.

Well, hell.

Libby could sense that everything had changed. She felt guilty. Why should she feel guilty? Somebody had to be her first. "Yes," she slowly answered.

"Damn."

Aron backed off, even more. She reached to pull him back, but he evaded her touch. Embarrassed, Libby let her hands drop.

"I don't do innocents, love. I refuse to be the one to besmirch your virtue."

Besmirch? Besmirch? "What if I want to be besmirched?" she questioned, more disappointed than she ever thought she could be about anything.

"I'm sorry, Baby Girl." Aron put his hat back on and gently picked her up off the counter and sat her down. "You don't know what you're asking." With those last sad words, he turned and walked away.

Chapter Three

What had happened? When she realized Aron was really walking away from her, she immediately felt bereft and cold. He didn't do innocents? Well, hell. Tears welled up in her eyes. She hadn't realized that inexperience could be such a turn-off to a man. It must be like getting a job. You had to have experience to get one, but nobody wanted to be the one to give you the chance at getting the experience. Maybe if she were prettier. Libby didn't really have a handle on her own sex appeal. She didn't have any idea if there was anything about her that would appeal to a man. At first, Aron seemed taken with her, but that might have been an act. Maybe, he was just the kind that liked to tease. Well, the joke was on her. She was left achy and empty, her breasts were swollen and sore and her feelings felt like someone had taken them out and stomped on them.

Mechanically, she went through the motions to ready everything for the next day's meals. She had decided earlier that gumbo and grilladas would be just the thing. They were dishes she could put on early in the day and the longer they cooked, the better they would be. With a heavy heart, she also carried out Bess's directive concerning Aron. She mixed up a batch of sweet roll dough so he could have hot cinnamon rolls with his coffee. Checking everything one last time, she started for bed. She could hear the McCoy brothers while they were watching television, and it sounded like they were having the time of their life.

Turning out the lights, she avoided the voices coming from the den and hastily made her way up the stairs to the haven of Bess's room. Throwing herself on the bed, she let the tears flow. Rats! How was she supposed to face Aron now? He had awakened every cell in her body to untold delights, and then he had just walked away. Looking around, she felt as if the room was trying to close in on her. God, she had to get outside! She couldn't stand to stay in the house one more minute. Where could she go? She needed to cool off and she could think of only one solution – the stock tank she had spied earlier would be just the thing. If Aron didn't want her, she would just wash his touch right off of her body. There wasn't anything wrong with her. Was there? She didn't have a swimsuit, but no one would follow her. Least of all Aron, as he didn't want to have anything to do with her.

***

Aron was miserable. Quaking with desire, he tried to walk off the hard-on that was still trying to warp his zipper. He had done the right thing. It didn't feel like it, but he had done the right thing. He wanted to feel Libby in his arms more than he wanted his next breath, but there was no way he was getting involved with someone who would expect something from him, something he wasn't prepared to give.

He fled the house, trying to find someplace where he could get Libby off his mind. Lord, he could still see her face; he could still feel the softness of her skin.
40

Damn, he had hurt her. Needlessly. Why had he come on so strong? He had acted like a randy fool. Who would have thought she would be an innocent? Hell, if he slept with Libby now, she would start picking out china patterns and wallpaper samples. No, it was better to cut it off before the whole mess got out of hand.

Aron retreated to his studio. This was his sanctuary. After he'd graduated college and retired from the rodeo circuit, he had been hungry for something to do besides just running the ranch. Through an odd series of events, sculpture had become his focus. Aron needed an outlet for his energy and he had always enjoyed working with his hands. During one of his trips to Mexico to check breeding stock, he had met Degas Santiago, a rich rancher who was also a sculptor. The man had intrigued him. While attending a party to meet the countries Ambassador to the United States, he had spent the night at Degas's home and he had graciously shown him around his studio, allowing Aron to try his hand at molding a piece of clay. Much to his surprise, he found he had a knack for it. Now, several galleries would buy every piece he could turn out. He could still remember the first sculpture he had ever made; it had been a horse standing on an outcropping of rock. The muscles of the animal were delineated and one could see every hair in its mane. He had called the horse, Freedom. What made it even more important was that he had made it for his mother. She had been over the moon about it. Then, he had lost her.

After the accident which had stolen his parents. Aron had immersed himself in work and family, but he had still taken the time to sculpt. He'd needed the distraction, especially when escaping Sabrina had been the only way to hold on to his sanity. The first showing he had participated in had been held in tandem with the

41

State Fair Rodeo in Dallas. It had been a simple misunderstanding, but someone had bought that piece right out from under his nose. The director of the exhibit had not distinguished Freedom as being a for-exhibit-only piece and the saleslady had sold it in error. The price had been right, but Aron would give his right arm to get it back. At first, he had been angry. But it was an honest mistake. Ever since then, he had been on the lookout for it. Rodeo people were a pretty close knit group, and one day he would cross paths with the person who had bought what he never intended to sell. The buyer had paid cash however, so it was like looking for a needle in a hay stack.

Tonight, he sat in the dark in his studio. For the first time, Aron found it was not a haven…it was damn lonely. The king-size bed over in the corner beckoned to him. How he would love to see Libby Fontaine draped across it, naked as the day she was born. Shit! All he wanted to do was march back over to the main house, find Libby, and hold her soft, little body tight in his embrace. He would kiss her over and over and then; he would allow his steel-hard cock to sink into the rich velvet of her womanhood. But that wasn't meant to be. Libby deserved a husband who loved her and children who adored her. He could offer her neither of those things, so it was better that he offered her nothing at all.

A splash outside the window of his second story studio alerted him that something was messing around the stock tank. Aron couldn't imagine what. There was nothing corralled in that lot; all of the horses and cattle were grazing out in the pasture land or they were shut up in the barn. What in the world?

He looked. He saw. He ached.

Libby walked up to the stock tank, trailing her hand in the cool, clear water. The glow from the security light was bright enough that he could see her quite clearly.

The night was still enough that he could hear her sigh. She held the towel together over her breasts; her legs were long and sleek and bare. Moonlight gave the pale skin of her arms and legs an iridescent quality. She could have been a wood nymph that had come out to play. Aron was totally enchanted. How he had walked away from this sweet thing was one of life's great mysteries. Midnight dark hair hung to her waist in thick, spiral curls. For a few tense minutes, Aron forgot to breathe.

The towel dropped.

Aron groaned.

Underneath that towel was nothing but beautiful, smooth, creamy skin. God in heaven, she was nude! Gloriously, magnificently nude! How long had it been since he had seen a naked woman outside of the pages of a magazine? Too long. Way, too damn long. And no woman he had ever been with had looked like this one. The clothes she had encased herself in ought to be taken out back and burned. They were a sacrilege to nature. Nothing should ever hide those luscious hills and valleys from his hungry eyes.

Libby still had her back to him. It appeared she was trying to figure out how to climb into the tank. There was a ladder about twenty feet to the left of her, but if he called out that information he would give himself away and she would vanish from his sight like a frightened fairy. She placed her hands on the rim of the tank and tried to pull her little self up and over. Partially successful, she managed to get her incredible tush elevated so that he could see a sweet little vee and past that – paradise.

Aron couldn't help but smile as he listened to her little grunts as she exerted herself. She wasn't very strong and soon she dropped back to the ground with a disappointed huff. Aron rubbed his palms on his denim-covered knees, aching to rub them over the tempting curve of her bottom.

"Turn around, Baby. Turn around." At that moment, he would have gladly given his share of Tebow to see her breasts. "Turn around, Sweetheart, lest I die," he whispered.

The Lord giveth…blessed be the name of the Lord. Libby turned and bent to pick up the towel. Twin globes of perfection hung down like the most delicious melons. Sweet Jesus! Honey-dews! Aron licked his lips, imagining how it would feel to claim those beauties, massaging them until she arched her back in ecstasy. He opened his mouth, slightly, as if in anticipation of fitting his lips over those incredible swollen tips. He was in lust! Deep, intense, nerve shattering lust! Aron had never been privileged to suckle on nipples as large as hers. Sabrina's nipples had been stingy, just like the rest of her. But Libby had nipples that were pink and puffy, just begging to be tongued and sucked.

Never before had he faced the possibility of erupting like a geyser without a single touch from his own hand or anyone else's. Unzipping his fly, Aron freed his enormous cock, seeking to gain some relief.

There was no way in hell that he was going to be able to stay away from her. She was the most tempting, succulent goddess he had ever been privileged to pay homage to. Walking around the tank, he heard her satisfied little exclamation when she finally found the ladder. In just seconds, she was up and over and the splash made him shiver. How he longed to cover her body like those warm, lucky waters.

Smiling, he watched her frolic in the water. Right by herself, she laughed and played. Aron wondered if she was lonely. Surprisingly, he wanted to know. Seeing her enjoy these few, stolen moments after the difficult

44

day she had endured, tugged at places in his heart that he had thought were out of commission. Unable to resist, he placed one hand on the windowsill and the other on himself and began stroking. Aron rested his chin on his forearm, captivated by her beauty and charm.

Then the game changed. Completely.

Libby began to touch herself.

Hypnotized, his mouth fell open as he gazed at her in rapt admiration. He watched her lean back on the rim and raised her body in a float. Aron had to bite his lip to keep from crying out when she cupped her own breasts and began to caress the tender mounds. Mesmerized, he watched her shape them and coax them into bountiful little mountains of gorgeous female flesh. When she began to pull on her nipples, stretching them out and milking them between her fingers, his hips bucked, begging to be allowed to join in the party. It wasn't just a few half-hearted tugs, Libby seemed to relish the attention she gave her tits. Apparently, she had spent a great deal of time practicing this particular skill, and God, if Aron had been called upon to judge her performance, he would have given her a perfect 10.

Aron was holding himself firmer now, getting more and more excited by the second, pumping his cock in long, smooth strokes. Libby's sensual little performance had him leaking pre-cum and a raging eruption wasn't far off. God, it was good! He imagined joining her in the warm water, slipping up close and covering one of those luscious nipples with his eager lips. God, he would suck and slurp, devouring all of that precious womanly flesh like a starving man presented with a T-bone steak. Damn!

Aron's breath hung in his throat when he watched one hand slip down past her waist to the dark little patch of curls. Her fingers curled and dipped, rhythmically working on her sweet spot. She thrashed in the water, trying to stay afloat, even while her legs and hips pumped in absolute abandon. Aron's hand kept up with her erotic dance, his own level of excitement reaching plateaus that he had rarely ever scaled.

Then, the world stopped turning. Aron knew that if he died at that moment, he would have no regrets. Libby's enjoyment sent him roaring off the cliff, flying apart in ecstasy. Huge plumes of cum sprayed up and over the windowsill, raining down the side of the barn. Never had he climaxed with such a violent explosive force. His eyes never left her, his ears were attuned to every word she screamed. And if he lived to be a hundred, he would never forget the sound of her husky little voice. For as Libby Fontaine brought herself to a glorious completion, it was his name she had shouted. "Aron! Aron! Oh, God, Aron, I want you so much!"

A broad smile overspread his relaxed features, while drops of sweat stood on his brow. At that moment, there was nothing in heaven or on earth that would have prevented him from going to her. All logical thought fled his mind. His body was clamoring with a need that took him completely over. Even though he had just experienced an incredible climax, Aron's thirst to taste her hadn't been quenched. He was already harder than he had ever been in his life. Hastily he made himself decent, putting his still excited rod back in his shorts. With shaking hands, he fastened his jeans and with his belt still hanging open, he went to join her. As he rounded the corner of the barn, he heard the splashing sound of her body emerging from the water.

When Libby pulled herself up the ladder, she found herself face to face with Aron. A hastily indrawn breath was the only sound she could make. Had he seen her? Had he heard her cry his name in the midst of her passion? Mortified, she turned to leap back into the darkness of the water.

"No, no, Baby." Aron reached out and grasped her wrist. "Don't run away from me, Bathsheba. You tempt me beyond what a mortal man could ever hope to resist." He pulled her forward and licked off the droplets of water that hung from the tips of her nipples.

The touch of his lips on her breasts made her pleasure center go molten. This sudden turn of events had Libby's head spinning. Aron was here! But, what did that mean? Leaning back away from his potent tongue, she crossed her hands over her breasts, and hung her head, not knowing what to think. Was this just another game? Would he tease her for a few more minutes, then walk away? Everything within screamed for her to open her arms and fit her wet body to his large, warm frame, but she didn't want to be pushed away for the second time.

"Don't hide from me, Libby." Aron pulled at her arms, revealing the luscious body that he craved more than food or air. "As much as I want to take you right here where we stand, we've got to talk. Will you come upstairs with me, to my studio?" He picked the towel up from where she had left it and gently wrapped it around her body, for the moment covering the precious treasure he coveted with every fiber of his being.

"Talk? You want to talk?" Libby's mind wasn't working very well. Still, there was no way she could ever turn him away. She had wanted him way too long to miss an opportunity to spend time with him.

Before he could answer her question, she appeared to make up her mind and held out her arms to him, and he gratefully picked her up. With one hand under her knees, he clasped her close, and quickly walked to the back stairs of the barn.

Every step he took, he kissed the top of her head, and she gave into instinct and nestled her cheek into the strong muscles of his shoulder. "Have you changed your mind about wanting me?" Libby couldn't help but ask.

"Oh, Babe," he tenderly answered, "there was never any question about my wanting you."

Kicking open the door of his studio with one booted foot, Aron deposited her gently onto his bed, flipping on the bedside lamp so he could see her clearly. His fantasy from earlier had blessedly come to life.

She ran her palm down his cheek, enjoying the coarseness of his whiskers. "Will you make love to me now?"

Everything within him clamored to take her up on what she offered—right damn now. Hell, being chivalrous was torture. "Libby, I have to say something first." Aron hesitated, not knowing how to proceed.

What she said next floored him.

"Is being a woman's first lover more trouble than it's worth? Is it not pleasurable for a man?"

Her innocence humbled him. Before he could reassure her, she continued to speak.

"Would it be better for you if I found someone else to…deflower me?"

With one forceful move, she was flat on her back and he was on top of her. "Hell, no! Your first time is a precious gift, and the man lucky enough to introduce you to the pleasures of love making will be one damn lucky son-of-a-bitch. I can only imagine that sharing your first experience would be heaven on earth for me. After all, I bet you're going to be soft and sweet and tight enough to drive me mad." Aron was kissing down her neck and all across the tops of her breasts. "So if there's any damn deflowering to be done, I'll be the one to take care of it." His ferocious look sent the once serious Libby into a spate of giggles.

Her spunky personality began to emerge. "Well, I hate to put you out. After all, I know how busy you are." She pretended to try to roll away from him and he tightened his grip on her until she could barely breathe.

"Hold on, Libby. Let me be serious for just a minute. Okay?" He rubbed his nose up and down her cheek, inhaling her clean, sweet smell. Surrendering to him completely, she lay back, allowing him to look deep into her eyes. "If we're going to do this, I need for you to understand something."

"Okay." Libby held her breath. What was he talking about?

"I can't offer you anything." As he said the words, somehow they didn't ring true in Aron's mind.

"What do you mean?" Was he talking money? Surely not. Or, maybe – white lace and wedding bells? She didn't have any use for either.

"I mean that I'm not making you any promises. I don't want anything permanent. I don't ever intend to marry again, so what we have will be just…" He groped for the right word. He hated to sound crass; after all she was an innocent.

"Sex." She supplied the word for him.

All right, she understood the score, but that didn't tell the full story. Aron stilled himself, waiting to see what her reaction would be. Would she push him off of her and leave in a huff? Would she start to cry? God, don't let her cry.

For a moment, there was only silence.

Then, she shocked him again, right down to the soles of his feet.

"That sounds just about perfect to me. Just sex. Yes, I believe that will fit right into my plans." Her expression was calm, as smooth and serene as the surface of a Hill Country lake.

Aron narrowed his eyes and tried to decide what species of femininity he was holding. "What did you say?" he growled.

Libby giggled again. Give a man what he asked for and he still wasn't happy. "I said that 'just sex' would work for me. I don't—I can't make any promises either. My future is uncertain at this point and anything of a permanent nature is out of the question." She spoke slowly, carefully weighing each word. She didn't want to ever lie to Aron, but she intended to walk away without him ever knowing about the cancer.

"So, let me get this straight..." He had to make sure.

"Good, Lord." Libby laughed. "I want you, Aron. Will you make love to me already?"

"Hell, yeah!" Who was he to question the beneficent goodness of the Almighty? What a gift this woman was! He moved to her side and turned her to face him. "Let's kiss some more."

Immediately, she draped one leg over his hips and scooted impossibly close. "That sounds wonderful. Your kisses are sweeter than Mounds candy."

"Hey, if we're talking candy bars, I'd rather be an Almond Joy instead of a Mounds." Lord, he enjoyed picking at her. She was more fun than a barrel of monkeys.

"What's the deal?" She played back. "They're both coconut!"

"Yeah," he said as he nipped at her chin. "But Almond Joy has nuts, Mounds don't." She squealed as he pinched her on the butt cheek. "And if you'll slip your little hand between my legs, I'll prove to you which category I fall into."

"Oh, you are too much." Excitement flashed through Libby's body. This time she didn't wait for Aron, she fisted her hand in his hair and pulled his head to hers.

He was hypnotized. Closing his eyes, he welcomed the magic. Libby took the tip of her tongue and teased him. Sweeping from one side of his mouth to the other, she coaxed him into giving her entrance. Aron played hard to get. This didn't put Libby off a bit; she just became more determined.

Opening her lips, she used her teeth to gently scrape and nibble all around his mouth. The feel of his beard stubble was making her quiver. Dipping her hips toward him, she playfully pressed her aching center up against his granite hard ridge.

When she ground against him, Aron's passion exploded. He thrust his tongue into her honeyed warmth and kissed her voraciously. Pushing her onto her back once again, he held her hands up over her head. "There is no way in hell you are unschooled!" he challenged. "You are blowing my mind!"

"I've read hundreds of erotic romances when I couldn't do anything else," she softly confessed, conspiratorially. "And I practiced. With a cucumber."

"You stuck a cucumber up your…?" he feigned horror.

"No." Libby was giggling so hard, she could barely catch her breath. "I sucked on it, so I would know how to…"

And that was as far in her explanation as she got. Aron reached between them and pulled her body free of the towel, then he kissed his way from her lips, past her chin and then to the valley between her breasts. "I'll let you show me what you've learned with the cucumber a little later, but right now I've got to latch my lips onto these sweet little tits. When I saw you getting excited right in front of my eyes at the dining room table, I almost came in my shorts." He plumped both breasts together, pushing the nipples close so he could trail his tongue from one to the other. "You have got the prettiest nipples," he crooned. "Watch." Fascinated, she saw him take a whole nipple and areola in his mouth and suck on it like a child would the top of an ice cream cone. She couldn't keep her eyes open however, for the pleasure was so intense she thought she might pass out.

"Oh, Aron," she gasped. "That feels so good." Libby couldn't contain herself; she undulated in his grasp, but he just latched on harder. Greedily, he lapped and sucked on her as if she were life-giving ambrosia from the gods. He made pleasurable noises in his throat while he ringed the hard nubbins with his tongue, feasting on her like there was no tomorrow. "I fantasized how your beard would feel rubbing against my skin." At her whispered description, Aron demonstrated to her that while the fantasy was good, reality topped it by about a thousand percent. Soon, her hips were bucking upward, seeking any kind of release. Realizing she was in need, Aron slid one hand down to her mons.

"I could suck on your breasts for hours, but it seems to me there are other parts of your body that are demanding attention." Aron was in heaven. He had never had so much fun making love. Sabrina had been a stingy lover, and he had been forced to make do with stingy bouts of sex—few and far between. Never had she lifted her hips, begging him wordlessly for his touch. When he slipped his fingers past the apex of Libby's thighs, he was met with a welcoming heat. She was wet for him. "You do want me, don't you?"

"Yes, please, Aron." She opened her legs wider. He didn't even have to ask. Before she knew what to expect, he had slid down her body, kissing his way to her navel. There he stopped to minister to the tiny well, afraid it would feel left out on his epic journey. With stingless bites, he nibbled his way down her tummy, stopping to blow a raspberry, just to hear the sweetness of her laugh. Then she stopped laughing.

"Oh, my Lord," she prayed. He was kissing her there! Never had she felt anything like it; never had she even imagined anything like it.

With his wide hands, he held her open, then he made himself at home. He lapped at her cream like a happy tomcat, smiling to himself as he heard her groan with pleasure.

"Do you like that?" he asked as he settled down to the task in earnest. Lifting her hips with his hands, he kissed from hipbone to hipbone, stopping in the middle to worship her, giving her clit a quick little lick.

"Yes!" she purred. "More!"

"Patience," he teased. Aron drove his tongue as deep into her channel as he could, then he proceeded to tongue-fuck her, "You taste so good, Libby," he praised her as he licked his way back to the pearl that peeked out from its little hood, like a shy child waiting to see if it would be invited to play. "Hold on, Baby. I'm going to make you feel good. You're going to like this." He proceeded to do as he promised and he had to forcibly hold her down.

Hot waves of joy rained down upon her, searing her with bolts of molten white electricity. Oh, she had cum, but always by her own hand, never by the talented tongue of the man she—even in the mindless frenzy of orgasm, she wouldn't let her mind say the words. A scream of rapture burst from her lips, and a shocking thrill of pleasure bloomed like fireworks in her brain. "Aron!"

He licked his way up her body, rejoicing in the tremors of her climax. "Are you protected, Libby?" God, please say yes. Aron couldn't stand the thought of sheathing himself with a synthetic barrier. He wanted to feel every iota of her being.

"I'm on the pill," she panted. "Boy scout."

Again, she made him laugh. "Don't you mean, girl scout?"

"No, I took the pill because I was scouting for boys."

"You'd better not be scouting anymore, Sweetheart." He tickled her up and down her ribs, while she wiggled and squiggled with joy.

Finally, face to face, they quieted. "I've found what I was looking for." She brushed a soft strand of hair from his forehead. "At least, until it's time for me to go," she reassured him with a reverent kiss over each eyelid.

Aron hugged her close, then once more parted her thighs and caressed her silky folds with a soft touch. "I'm going to stretch you just a little bit. I don't want to hurt you. I want it to feel good." Trusting him, she laid back, allowing him to do as he wished. But, then, she eyed that white shirt with the snaps and grinned. No better time than the present to make that particular day dream come true. She placed her hands on the lapels of his shirt and pulled hard. It parted as easily as if she had said, 'Open Sesame'. To give him credit, he didn't look very surprised. Maybe he was used to being ravished.

"My Word," she marveled. "Look at this chest!" He was utterly magnificent. Crisp dark hair covered flesh that just begged to be petted. Little brown nipples looked in dire need of being kissed and miles of muscles seemed to scream for her to map them with eager fingers.

At the determined look in her eye, he paused in what he was doing – just to wonder at her fascination with his beat-up old body. "Make yourself at home. What is mine is yours." He thought about just laying back and letting her enjoy herself. Finally, the call of his desperate cock won out, and he started back to working at her pussy in earnest, readying her softness for his possession. All the while, she entertained herself by stroking his chest and tonguing his nipples, nipping and kissing every inch of him she could reach. Had he ever experienced anything like her before? He didn't think so. Libby was a wonder. She seemed to crave him. Him. Aron wasn't used to reciprocal attention. The sex he had participated in had mostly been one-sided, vaguely satisfying, but nothing to write home about. This...this was a whole different ball game. Libby wasn't just participating; she was recruiting, coaching and leading the cheers.

What Aron was doing south of her equator finally captured her attention, causing her worship of his chest to slow down a bit. As his fingers pushed up inside of her, she drew in a breath and held it. Oh, his fingers felt so much better than her own ever could have. For one thing, they were longer and fatter...and then they were his, which made all the difference.

He began a rhythmic invasion of her femininity with one finger, until she was squirming with pleasure. Two fingers and she sought his lips, needing to connect with the one who was bringing her such joy. His question came out of the blue. "Have you ever put a toy of any kind inside you, Libby?"

"No," she answered between kisses. "I've worn tampons, I'm okay."

"I'm slightly bigger than a tampon, Sugar." He continued to press into her, adding a third finger to the mix. Hurting her was not an option. But if the heat she was producing and the little whimpers and purrs coming from her sweet lips were any indication of her excitement, she was ready for him. Still, he pushed her toward another climax. It was best to be sure.

Virginal, she might be, but she still caught on to what he was doing. "Aron, no. Stop! I don't want to come, yet. I want to wait until you're inside me. I want to wait for you." She tried, in vain, to hold off the impending climax. "I'm going to use up all of my orgasms." She truly seemed dismayed.

Chuckling he kissed her, even as he deepened the sensual assault. "God loves girls more than he does boys, Libby. He made you so that you could come over and over again. It's just us poor unfortunate males who have to wait and recuperate." Aron punctuated his words with kisses to her face and neck. "So, don't fret. Let me hear you. Purr for me, Kitten. Come for me. Don't hold back." Latching on to one nipple, he gloried in her response as she rode his hand to nirvana.

Libby was literally gulping for air. Never had she envisioned pleasure like she was receiving from Aron. Then a thought occurred, "Roll over," she demanded. How could she have forgotten this? It would be like going to Florida and missing Disneyworld.

"What?" he asked in a daze. He was past ready to claim her. His penis was strutted with passion and anxious to enter the Promised Land.

"I've got to get a look at you." She pushed at his shoulder, trying to get him to lie flat.

"What?" he asked again. There wasn't enough blood in his brain to allow him to comprehend her request.

"I want to see you, all of you. Especially your joystick." Libby was serious.

"You're killing me, Libby." Aron didn't know whether to laugh or cry. She maneuvered herself from underneath him and he moaned with frustration.

"You've still got most of your clothes on. How did that happen?" In the blink of an eye, she set to work undressing him. His shirt was hanging open, his belt was
56

unbuckled, but other than that, he was fully dressed. "We've got to get your boots off, first." Helpless, he lay back and watched her work. Here he was, as hard as a rock, and she was gallivanting around like a butterfly. She did have a point about the clothes, though. Finding a reserve of strength, he began to help her undress him. Aron was easily distracted, however, by the sway of her breasts and the cute little dimples on her bottom. When she had him down to his shorts, she sat up beside him like it was Christmas morning and she was waiting to open a gift under the tree.

With wide eyes, she gently traced the outline of his stiff cock. Aron swore he had never swelled to such proportions before. A lot of things were different with Libby—the laughter, the passion, the sheer joy one could find in another's body. Glancing at him, as if in permission, she began the unveiling.

Getting up on her knees, she straddled his legs, so that she was sitting over his calves. Grasping the waistband of his boxer briefs, she tugged down—and out he sprang in all of his glory. "Look at him!" she exclaimed with joy. "Aron, he's so beautiful!"

He didn't know whether to laugh or moan when she leaned over and grabbed him with both hands. She began kissing him from tip to root, all up one side and down the other. Any other time he would have been gung-ho for her enthusiasm, but right now he was about to go all Mount St. Helens on her. He put a hand down to pull her up, when she placed one more soft, sweet kiss right on the weeping tip end. "You are remarkably, wonderfully made." She kissed him again, quoting from one of her favorite novels.

That was it. He couldn't take anymore. Grasping her by the waist, he flipped her up and over. She squealed in surprise, as he got her into position. "No more teasing Love, or the game is going to be over before the quarterback even gets on the field." Spreading her thighs, he maneuvered himself over her.

"Are you heading into the end zone?" she queried with a straight face as he settled his body down onto her, pushing the blunt end of his cock into the gate of her tender opening.

He was so thick; she didn't know how in the world her body would ever accommodate him.

"Going for a touchdown." He grinned as he pressed forward a half-inch. Suddenly, the sensation overwhelmed him. He hadn't ridden bareback since way before Sabrina. She hadn't wanted to feel his naked cock inside of her. She'd said she couldn't stand the way it felt when he came inside her body. He couldn't imagine Libby ever saying such a thing. His eyes rolled to the back of his head. Sweet Jesus! Ecstasy! She was warm, wet, silky, tight, and as soft as the inside of a cream puff. "I'll never last," he moaned.

"Aron, give me your hands." He looked down and she was holding her hands up, wanting to weave their fingers together. He sat up and pulled her hips up and over his thighs. Pressing forward he managed to push another inch inside of her. Giving her what she wanted, he held her hands, and then he began to pump. Libby was incredibly snug, squeezing his organ like a tight little vice. Watching her face, he looked for any sign of discomfort, but all he could see was happiness, pleasure and a hunger he had never seen on a woman's face before. "More, Aron. Give me more," she urged him on.

He didn't have to be asked twice; he pushed steadily into her until he was buried to the hilt. Then, he had to stop for a second. The pleasure was just too intense. Miraculously, she was making these tiny little movements deep down inside, massaging and clasping him with her sheathe. "Are you ready?" he asked, hoping to high heaven she would say 'yes'.

"Please, please," better than yes. Way better. Still holding her hands, he pushed them over her head and began driving into her with an unrelenting linear motion. Soon, they were both grunting and moaning with delight. "Oh, that's good, Aron, so good." She pushed her breasts into the air, begging him to suck her nipples.

He was a talented guy; he could do two things at once, so he granted her mute request. Teasing, he nipped her and she bucked upward with delight. "Oh, I like that!" she moaned.

"Oh, you Doll." he praised her as he prepared to adore her other breast. "You like everything."

"I like you, Aron McCoy," she exhaled in a rush, another orgasm barreling down on her like a freight train.

"I like you, too, Libby." Too much, maybe. As she reached her peak, the tiny flutters of her pussy around his cock almost sent Aron into orbit. The sexy little sounds she made as the ecstasy rolled through her body nearly did him in. He had to hold on, just a little more, it was just too good to stop. "Come on, Baby, that's the touchdown...let's go for the extra point." He urged her on, gyrating his hips, nudging her cervix, searching to give her all the pleasure he could. The sound of his balls slapping her bottom in a jungle beat only spurred him to increase his driving speed. Never in his life had he experienced sex like this. Where had she been all of his life?

Libby was incoherent with pleasure as he kept pushing her to accept more, and she was only too glad to take what he dished out. "Sweet Lord," she whispered as she arched her back, pushing as much of her breast as she could into his mouth. The harder he sucked, the more she wanted. She knew she liked to read about sex, but she had no idea she would be such a glutton when it came to the real thing. It was Aron. He was the reason. No other man could possibly affect her this way.

His body stiffened as he neared his climax, the pleasure so intense he thought the top of his head might blow off. He mindlessly thrust into her creamy depths, her little body a welcome port to his marauding demands. Flashing, crashing bombardments of ecstasy pummeled into him with a fiery culmination. He abandoned himself to bliss, letting all of the tension of four years of discontent and celibacy flow out of him. He cried out his deliverance as he released great jets of cum deep within her. His eyes never left her face, she was so beautiful. Closing her eyes in ecstasy, her body kept moving, milking him, clasping him, begging for more. At last, in absolute contentment, he stretched out over her, covering her, claiming her. She might not realize it, but Libby Fontaine had come to his rescue.

She held him close, stroking his back, just listening to him breathe. "Thank you Aron, that was unbelievable." Libby planted a small kiss on his shoulder. He was heavy as he lay on her, pressing her down, but she welcomed his weight. It made her feel precious and wanted—for a little while, at least.

Her words of appreciation roused him from his lethargy. "Thank you, Sweetheart. You don't know it, but you broke a drought for me. It's been four long years since I've had sex."

Four years? Libby didn't know what to think. Sheesh! Any port in a storm—all horses are grey in the dark—anybody would appeal after four years. "Four years? I can't believe an exciting man like you would ever do without sex for that long," she spoke carefully.

What the hell, Aron decided to get in touch with his feelings and open up. "My ex-wife, she did a real

60

number on me; she burned me, spurned me and hung me up to dry. It's taken me this long to trust a woman enough to get this close." He realized what he had said. "I guess that means I trust you, Libby."

"I'm glad, Aron. I won't abuse your trust. We'll keep what happened within these walls our secret. The other boys will never know it even occurred." She brushed her lips once more over his shoulder and pushed lightly so he would let her up. "I guess I need to go to my room, the alarm clock will go off pretty early. I'm going to try and beat all of you up by at least an hour."

"Hold on." Aron stopped her from moving. "I don't intend to flaunt our relationship in front of Nathan, he's too young. But I don't care if he knows there's something going on between us...that we're seeing one another, sort of. As far as the rest of those yahoos go, I want them to know that I've roped you, hog-tied you, branded you and fenced you in my spring-fed pasture. From now on, as far as they're concerned, you belong to me."

"Tag?" she asked with a smile.

"Exactly, I don't want them getting any ideas. They know I don't ever intend to remarry, but they can't expect me to be a monk for the rest of my life, either. They'll understand. And, what we did tonight...well, I intend to do it twice a day and four times on Sunday." As he said those words, he punctuated them with kisses until she was writhing beneath him in a fit of giggles. "Sweetheart, you just gave me the best ride I could ever imagine, and I have no intention of it being a once-in-a-lifetime event." He finished off by blowing on her stomach like he would a toddler.

She flung her arms around his neck and hung on. "Thank you. That's what I wanted, too. I wasn't going to ask for it, though. I didn't want you to think I was making any demands."

Climbing from the bed, Aron pulled on his jeans. He held his shirt up for her to wear, since all she had worn to the stock tank had been a towel. That hit him sort of funny. "I can't believe you snuck out of the house in only a towel!"

"You had me all hot and bothered, all I could think about was cooling off," she admitted.

"Cover up more next time, Baby Doll. I'm the only man I want looking at your body." Before she could answer, he picked her up and stalked off.

"I can walk."

"Yes, you can, but you don't have to. You've got a big, strong man to carry you. Besides, you're barefoot; there might be grass burrs or snakes crawling around." At the word snake, she catapulted upward in his arms, almost draping herself around his neck. "Hey! Now I know what to say to make you snuggle closer. Afraid of snakes, are you?"

"Horribly, I can guess one could say—phobic." She was still shaking, just thinking about the horrible, slimy creatures.

"Good thing I'm tall then, they'd have to be on stilts to reach you up here or..." he snorted, "fall out of a tree on you." That elicited another movement in his arms, this time she burrowed into his chest and he just laughed some more. "You are so cute."

He propped her up on one knee while he opened the door, then locked it behind him. Carrying her up the stairs, he stole a few kisses on the way, just for good measure. When they passed Bess's room, she grunted and made a little motion with one foot. He just kept on going until he was behind closed doors. His bedroom door. Laying her on the bed, he set the alarm clock and went to the bathroom. Returning with a wet washcloth he wiped her off gently between the legs, then kissed her right dab on the clitoris, then moved up to kiss her right over her heart. She sighed sleepily, giving him a sweet smile. "Are you sure you want me to sleep in here with you?"

"This is where you will sleep from now on." He didn't even realize the implications of what he was saying.

"Until it's time for me to go," she added and he grunted noncommittally. That didn't sound right. Where in the hell did she think she was going?

Aron didn't even realize his mind was slowly changing.

Sable Hunter

Chapter Four

Aron knew he needed to sleep, but he couldn't resist just taking the time to look at her. She lay on her side and he was cuddled up against her back, nestled together like two sugar spoons. He had to grin though, because every once in a while she would push her little bottom back into his groin and wiggle it just a little. The first two times she did it, he thought she was awake and trying to start something sexy, but the little angel was asleep—fast asleep. That tempting little move was just her body's natural reaction to him. To him! She didn't want to sleep away from him—not touching during the night—like Sabrina. Libby was like a warm, soft kitten. She didn't mind being held and stroked. Occasionally, he would run the palm of his hand from her shoulder down her arm or from her waist over her hips, just acquainting himself with her body and its response to him. Slipping his arm under her head, he pulled her back so he could kiss her on the temple. When he did, she let out the softest, sweet, little breathy sigh. It made his heart turn over. God, was she real? Was she as sweet as she seemed to be? Could she be happy at Tebow away from the city lights and the malls? Could she be happy with one man, instead of a troupe like Sabrina required? All of these questions rolled through his head, until exhaustion allowed him to rest.

Much later, Libby pulled herself from Aron's arms. It was only four-thirty. When he pulled her back again, she rolled over and kissed him gently on the lips. "I'm getting up, you rest for another hour." With an incoherent little grunt, Aron snuggled down under the covers. Libby made her way back to Bess's room and into a warm, welcoming shower. She was sore in places that made her excited just thinking about them. Aron had loved her long and hard and she wouldn't have traded one second of it for the whole world. She knew there would come a day when this memory would get her through some dark, lonely hours.

It was so tempting to go back in and swipe a few more kisses; something told her she could probably interest him in even more if she tried. That was a heady feeling, sort of like a power trip. Sickly, little Libby Fontaine could make the great Aron McCoy sit up and beg. Well, maybe. He needed his rest, however, and she had a job to do.

The kitchen was a welcoming place. All of Tebow was warm and inviting, a huge log house with acres of exposed beams, golden oak flooring and huge stone fireplaces. It would take a lot of hours and hard work to keep this place spic and span. But, Libby would do it—gladly. But first, the cinnamon rolls. She popped them in the oven, made a strong pot of coffee and some sticky, ooey-gooey white icing for the rolls. Soon, a heavenly smell would rise to the rafters. While they were cooking, she prepared three gigantic frittatas with potatoes, eggs and sausage, and after, a pan of homemade biscuits. A noise from the pipes alerted her that someone was up—probably Aron. Quickly, she filled a tray with the rolls and the coffee and sat it at his place at the table. That way, if he wanted to take it to his office, it would be ready for him. She also ran outside, retrieved his newspaper, and placed it on the tray.

Although it was late summer, the air conditioner was turned down low. Inspiration struck and she hurried to the laundry room and found a thick fluffy navy blue towel. The oven was warm, so she rolled it up and laid it within the toasty confines for about ninety seconds. Testing it with her fingers, it was perfect. Hurrying up the stairs, she darted in his room and crept into his bathroom —prepared to lay it on his sink and then slip back out. Like a flash, without looking, she opened the door and stuck her hand in to deposit the warm offering. A hand gripped her hard, stopping any further movement. With one smooth swing, Aron pulled her in and right up against his naked, damp body. Covering her mouth, he began to feast. "What are you doing sneaking in on me, Angel? Were you warm for my form? " he joked.

'Yes, always,' she thought.

Reaching behind her, she pulled the towel and unfurled it, wrapping him in its soothing warmth. "Damn, that's nice." He enfolded her in his arms again; he would never tell her that the towel was in his way. Her body was much more welcome, but the thought of the toasty towel was one of the nicest things anybody had ever done for him. "Are you trying to spoil me?"

"I'm trying to pamper you," she said against his throat. Then, she pulled back. "My frittatas!" She yelped. "Hurry down, Aron. I have a surprise for you."

He watched her go with a smile. Suddenly the world was a much brighter place.

***

Aron closed his eyes in ecstasy. "These are the best damn things I have ever had in my mouth." A broad grin spread across his face. "Except for these..." He lunged for Libby, picking her up in his arms and fitting his mouth over one breast—bra, shirt and all.

"Aron, that's going to show," Libby gave a token protest. But, God it felt good. He applied suction and she felt her vagina contract in jealousy. Walking to the laundry room, with Libby wrapped around his waist, he continued to suckle at her breasts with vigor. When he sat her up on the dryer, there were big wet circles on her black T-shirt. "I don't have any more clothes down here," she whispered loudly.

Ignoring her anxiety, he fished out one of Nathan's shirts from the dryer. Turning to her, he started to divest her of the marked garment. When his eyes settled on the two wet circles, he felt his staff rise to the occasion. "Man, I've done myself in." Aron groaned as he stripped the soiled garment off, peeling her bra cups down and feasting in earnest. Libby cradled his head to her breast, thinking this had to be one of the sexiest things she could ever imagine. Laughter interrupted the romantic interlude. Not their laughter, it was coming down the stairs, and soon would come around the corner. Gently pulling the cups back up, he slipped Nathan's shirt over her head.

"What if they find us in here? What are you going to tell them?" she inquired, but he just smiled. Picking her up, he walked back into the kitchen.

When he stepped into the dining room, he planted another proprietary kiss on her lips, right in front of the whole family. The laughter stopped, the talking stopped, and you could have heard a pin drop, until Jacob sighed and said, "Well, hallelujah."

***

Libby made herself at home. She mopped floors;

she polished banisters and washed windows, always checking the horizon for one particular wide-shouldered cowboy. Having gotten up at four-thirty, she had moved several mountains by ten-thirty, so she allowed herself to venture outside and explore. The gumbo and grilladas were on simmer, so lunch and supper were practically done. She had asked Jacob if it would be all right to make a phone call to Bonnie Drake, the friend she had told Nathan about. Bonnie wasn't home, but she had left a message explaining what she needed to know. Bonnie would call back when she had time.

Hearing a horse whinny in the barn, she took off toward the beloved structure on winged feet. Forever she would treasure the sight of big old red barns, because one had been the sight of her most precious hours—becoming Aron's lover for the first time. Peeking inside the barn, she discovered that the occupant wasn't Aron, it was Joseph.

"Hey," he greeted her. "Want to get down and dirty with me?"

"Oh, yeah," Libby answered. Excited. Not sexual excitement, just plain old 'glad to be alive' excitement.

Aron, standing two stalls over, stilled in concern. Was history repeating itself? Walking softly, he slipped up on the two—one whom he loved, the other whom he was quickly beginning to worship. Instead of a risqué scene of two cheating people, he found his brother shoveling horse manure and his doll-face pushing the wheelbarrow. "Hey, Joseph, don't make the munchkin do the heavy work."

Seeing Aron, Libby launched herself at him, and he caught her easily. "I want to help. It's fun to muck around."

"What did you say?" He laughed, knowing what she said, but wanting to fluster her anyway. "It's fun to…what?"

Playfully, she punched him, then squeezed him tight. "I missed you."

Aron's heart tightened. He refused to analyze the situation; he just enjoyed it.

***

Libby worked with Joseph until a quarter to twelve, when she took off to make a pot of rice and pour the iced tea. All five of the older brothers worked the ranch. Jacob had told her that Tebow ran thousands of head of prime Beefmaster and Longhorn cattle. Right now, it was time to move the weaned calves and vaccinate them for Brucellosis. It was hard work, but at least they were close enough to all come in for lunch. The gumbo was chicken, sausage and shrimp, thickened with filet and rich with Creole spices. Libby had even made some pecan pralines for dessert. The Fontaines were all from New Orleans originally, so Libby had a whole plethora of Louisiana specialties.

"My God, it smells good in this house!" Isaac shouted. He bounded in, grabbed Libby and threw her in the air. Before he could catch her, she was gone. Aron had easily stepped up and stole her from his brother's clutches. It wasn't that he didn't trust Isaac, but Libby belonged to him. "Watch it. Be gentle with my girl." He sat her down and fixed her a bowl of gumbo himself. This was the second time he had served up her meal.

"Isaac, could you teach me how to drink and shoot pool?" Libby asked as Isaac and Aron both choked on their tea.

"What did you say?" Isaac asked her for clarification, his eyes locked with Aron's.

"Would you take me to a bar and teach me to shoot pool and maybe do tequila shots?" Innocence laced her voice, as she took small, delicate bites of the warm stew.

"Uh," was all Isaac managed to get out of his mouth, before Aron asked the obvious.

"Why in the world would you want to do something like that?" By God, if anyone was going to take her to a bar, it wouldn't be Isaac, it would be him.

"I have a lot to learn, and I only have a few months," she reminded him, knowing that they thought she meant here at Tebow—while she meant healthy.

"What do you mean?" Aron asked. "Why are you trying to cram a whole life time of living into just a few months?" Libby looked up and saw that Jacob was watching her closely. Crap! Finesse, Libby. Finesse.

"Well, my dream has always been to live on a ranch, and I'm here. I want to take advantage of the situation." She was careful at this point. "I'm also getting to do…other fun stuff." She bugged her eyes out at Aron, who grinned. "But I also want to walk on the wild side, just for a night or two. Who better to show me those things than Isaac?" It made perfect sense to Libby.

"If you want to go, I'll take you." Aron settled the matter. No argument.

Libby thought, 'we'll see'. "Are you sure you want to be seen in public with me? After all, I'm only a passing fanny." She was whispering, but every McCoy heard her.

Aron looked slightly uncomfortable. Libby was not a passing fancy or a passing fanny. "It's fancy, Libby…not fanny."

"Oh, the other made more sense, actually." She was serious. Cute, but serious.

"What do you mean, Libby?" Noah looked at his brother with censure in his eyes.

Shit! Aron hadn't wanted to deal with this in front of his brothers. "Just leave it, Noah," he ordered his

71

brother.

Libby instantly realized she had spoken out of turn. "I'm sorry," she whispered to Aron. "I just assumed they understood what's going on."

"Understood what?" Joseph asked.

"It's okay, Aron. Joseph, I don't want you to argue." Libby tried to repair the damages.

Aron looked at his bowl, not knowing whether to feel guilty or angry. He opted for angry. "It's just none of their business, Libby," he spoke softly, but sternly.

"Sorry," she murmured. Picking up her bowl, with only a few bites missing, she placed it on the counter and turned to run up the stairs.

"What have you done?" Jacob asked his brother, point-blank.

"Libby knows the score." Aron wouldn't meet his brother's eyes.

"You told her she was just a short, sleazy affair?" Jacob had stood up and walked over to his brother's chair.

"I didn't use the word sleazy." Aron bit off every word. "I just leveled with her. I explained that I wasn't interested in anything permanent, that I had no intention of remarrying and that I couldn't make her any promises."

"Classy, Aron, classy." Disappointment dripped off every word that Jacob spoke. "Don't you know that Libby is a keeper?"

"She said that a casual affair fit right in with her plans, that she couldn't make any promises, either." Even to Aron's own ears, his words sounded pitiful.

Jacob stood there for a moment, like he wanted to say something else. After a while, he just shook his head, sat back down and ate in silence.

"Go to her, Aron." Noah implored, all of their eyes cut to their big brother, hoping he would do the right thing. "She's such a sweet, little thing. You don't want to leave her crying up there all alone. She didn't do anything wrong."

Aron didn't argue with his brothers. They were right. Throwing down his napkin, he hurried to the stairs. Trust Libby to force the truth out in the open, even when he didn't want it there. He went to his room first, after all that's where he told her she belonged. She wasn't there. Next, he checked Bess's room. It was empty, also. A tingle of panic crawled down Aron's spine.

Heading out the back door, he started searching for her. He found her in the barn, brushing down Kismet, Jacob's Appaloosa. As she groomed the big horse, she talked to him. "You are so good-looking. Did you know that?" Moving behind the big horse, Aron held his breath. Kismet was a good animal, he never kicked, but you had to be careful when you put yourself in the reach of hard, deadly hooves. "I like to brush you. It makes me feel better." Aron started to go to her, but she continued to talk, so he listened. "I made Aron angry. I didn't mean to. I would rather cut off my finger." She moved on around the big horse, until all Aron could see of her was just the top of her head. "He's a good man. If things were different…" then her voice faded to a whisper. Aron couldn't stand it anymore. He walked up to Kismet, leaned over and picked her up.

Libby was startled. "Cheez-n-Crackers!" she yelped. The odd little saying almost made Aron cry. What was wrong with him? This one little woman was turning his world upside down. When she realized what was happening, she melted into him. "Don't be mad at me, I'm sorry. I'm so sorry. Aron, I was just trying to keep things light. I didn't know they would misunderstand."

When he felt dampness on his neck, he almost lost it. "I'm not mad, Libby. It's okay; it was all my fault, not yours. I can't expect you to know what's going on in my mind unless I tell you. All you knew was what I told you. Don't cry, Sweetheart. I can't stand it. Don't cry."

Trying to please him, she steeled herself and wiped her eyes. "From now on, I'll keep my mouth shut, I won't say anything. I promise. Coming between you and your brothers is the last thing I would ever want to do."

At once, Aron thought of Sabrina and the delight she took in causing trouble. She would be laughing right now, instead of tearfully begging his pardon. "Don't hold your tongue on my account. If I'm not man enough to stand by what I say, I don't need to say anything at all." He kissed the trail of tears from her cheeks.

"Can you tell me what I did wrong, so I can make sure to not do it again?" she hiccupped the question.

Blowing out a breath, Aron bit the bullet. He didn't want to hurt her any more than he already had. "They wanted what you and I have to be real. My brothers worry about me. It's their hope that I won't grow old all alone."

Leaning her head against his chest, she rubbed the material that covered his steel-hard pecs. "Tell them that it is real."

He grew very still.

She continued to speak. "For whatever time it lasts, it is real. That's no lie, not on my part anyway. I'm not pretending. I think you're the most wonderful man in the world, and I'm the luckiest woman to get to spend even one hour in your arms." He tightened his grip. "So tell them not to worry, while I'm here, I'll treasure you. And after I'm gone, you'll be so used to being loved, that you'll turn every cactus and rock upside down looking for someone to replace me."

Her words made his heart ache. He didn't really understand it, but the feeling was sharp enough to make him close his eyes in pain.

Replace her? Not a chance in hell

***

Everywhere he looked, Libby was there. He watched her running in the pasture with the horses and the dogs. She held her hands over her head, as if she was trying to catch the wind. That afternoon at supper, there was a jar of wildflowers sitting in the middle of the table. Libby had reheated the gumbo and at three o'clock she had carried each brother a steaming bowl. It had been her fault their lunch was disrupted and she didn't want them going hungry on her account.

Nathan had come bounding off the school bus at four o'clock and Libby met him at the bus stop. She helped him carry his books, as he munched on some warm chocolate chip cookies she had brought with her.

Aron watched from a distance. Libby was great with Nathan. She had gotten the name of a spell check program that would make Nathan's school work much easier for him. Noah had immediately ordered one and installed it on Nathan's laptop. The only problem that Aron could see was that Nathan was getting too attached to Libby too fast. He knew he could control his emotions—after all, he was a grown man, but Nathan was going to get hurt. He hated to do it, but he was going to have to speak to Libby about it.

***

"What are grilladas, Libby?" Nathan asked, even

75

as he shoveled them in.

"What do they taste like?" she challenged him to analyze the flavors.

"Beef and tomatoes." She nodded that he was right. "Onions and peppers and rice."

"That's most of it, but there's also broth, raisins, spices and Worcestershire sauce."

"Wortawhat?" Nathan laughed.

"It's a sauce made from lots of spices and also anchovies."

Six sets of cutlery clattered on the plates. "Anchovies?" Joseph looked dismayed. "I don't like anchovies."

"You can't taste them, can you?"

"No."

"Eat." Aron ordered. If they ate every time Aron ordered them to do so, they would be as big as horses.

Jacob wondered if he was the only one noticing that Libby was fast becoming an essential part of the family.

***

"Where are you going?" Aron watched Libby head toward the back door. He was about ready to go to bed. First, he wanted to warn her about Nathan, then he wanted to make love.

"I'm going to go milk the cow."

Hell, she was serious. "At ten o'clock? She'll be asleep." Aron almost whined. He was horny.

"I promised Jacob that I would do it at three, but I took everybody a bowl of gumbo, instead." Aron walked behind her as she purposefully strode to the barn. Libby acted like she lived here. Funny, Aron didn't mind at all.

Harrumph! He thought he had been the only recipient of the afternoon gumbo treat. He wanted to be special in Libby's eyes.

"Jacob said that the cow's tits hurt if she isn't milked regularly." Libby's words hit him right between the legs. Aron knew he was probably crazy, but Libby was turning him on with her udder talk.

"It's teats on a cow, Baby, not tits."

"Same thing."

Aron groaned.

"Why are you making funny rackets?"

"Because all your talk about teats and tits is stoking a fire inside of me, that's why. My dick is all awake and excited."

"Oh," Libby's voice went soft with excitement. "I'll milk fast, okay?" She got her stool and her bucket and she settled down to do as Jacob had instructed. Grasping the teats, she began to pull, rhythmically. Bossy swished her tail and Libby ducked. But she kept pulling on those cow teats, and the milk was filling the bottom of the bucket. The more she pulled, the more Aron remembered the night that he watched her milk and knead her own puffy little nipples. He watched for a few seconds more, then he growled. "Get up, Libby. My hands are stronger, I can do it faster."

She complied, but she fussed. "It was a learning experience, Aron. I wanted to do it."

"You're killing me, Sugar. I'll teach you everything you need to know—upstairs, in my bed. All I can think about is you pulling on your own nipples in that stock tank, and how I'm going to do the same thing to you in just a minute." His words effectively cooled her anger and heated her everywhere else. Soon, she found that her hips were moving in concert with the sound of the streams of milk hitting the side of the bucket. As Aron finished up, Libby walked over and locked every barn door. She pulled every shutter tight and secured every entrance. Then, she walked back to where Aron was rising and behind his back, she stripped down to her altogether.

Little hands crept around his waist and began to unfasten his buckle. "What are you doing?" Aron asked hoarsely.

"Giving us both what we want," she whispered in his ear as she nipped the lobe and licked him on the neck. Soon, he was as naked as she was, and God Almighty, he was fine. Perspiration glittered on every surface, delineating every bulge and ripple. Stepping up to him, she ran her fingers up his chest, through the crisp hair and around his nipples. Then, boldly, she bent down and cupped his sac. "Is tonight cucumber night?" she asked hopefully.

"No, too excited." Aron was honest. "I have something else in mind." Showing her what he meant, he put both hands at her waist and lifted. "Wrap your legs around me, Libby-sweet." The endearment warmed her heart.

All thoughts of Nathan and his request slipped Aron's mind for the moment. Taking her hips in his hand, he lifted her until her breasts were mouth level. "I wish you had milk, I'd suck you dry."

His words rushed right to her womb. To have milk, she would have to be pregnant. With his child. Glory be! What she wouldn't give for that to be true! He swirled his tongue around each nipple. Next, he scraped his teeth over them, nipping ever so slightly. It might be wrong, but Libby liked a bit of pain with her pleasure. It made her feel so alive. Traveling outward, he gave her little love bites all around each breast, stopping to mark her in a place that no eye but his would ever see. The deep suction made her hips move against him. "Suck my nipples. Please Aron, suck them hard." She almost smiled when she said that. How many times had she read that phrase in one of her erotic novels? And to think, now it was her turn to say it. Glory be! And when he did as she asked...the earth moved. She could swear it did. Nothing could beat the incredible sensation of a man's mouth at your breast. Womb-clinchers. That's what Aron's breast kisses were—womb-clinchers. She could feel every sharp pull all the way to her always-meant-to-be-empty womb. Despite the bite of sadness, she fell apart in his arms, quaking from one of the hardest orgasms she had ever experienced.

"Did you like that, Libby? You must have, you came so good. No woman has ever exploded for me like that, not just from my kisses on her breasts." Aron rewarded her with a few more. "You are so sweet. Now, let's get down to the business at hand."

He held her with one strong arm and guided his cock into her with the other. She was more than ready to receive him and gasped with awe as he impaled her on his thick rod. "Oh, yeah," she sighed in relief. "There is nothing in the world that feels better than you inside me." She kissed him on the neck. He was so strong. He didn't bother to back her up to the wall or anything, he just manually moved her up and down on his manhood, huffing his satisfaction with each pump. With admiration, Libby smoothed her hands over his shoulders, down his back and then watched in rapture as his beautiful butt clenched and unclenched with each thrust. He had magnificent legs and thighs. They were perfectly muscled and as thick and strong as tree trunks. There was no way she was going to be able to last very long at this rate. Why should she try? After all, God loves girls best, that's what Aron told her. As she swan-dived off the cliff of rapture, Libby wondered how in God's name would she ever live a day without him.

In. Out. In. Out. God, she tightened on the down

stroke, causing the sides of her channel to provide enough friction to drive him bonkers. "Libby, I could make love to you forever. Sweetheart, you are so good." Her full faith and trust was in him. She didn't resist, or fear a fall. Never had a woman been as free with herself as Libby. She was a wonderful gift, an undeserved wonderful gift. Out of the blue, she had walked into his life and proved to him that not all women were selfish bitches; some were sweet angels with broken wings. As he pumped into her relentlessly, letting his climax overtake him, Aron decided that he wanted to know just why Libby thought a future between them wasn't possible. Not that he wanted a future with her, mind you. But, he wanted to know.

"You are an incredible lover, Aron." Libby lay on his shoulder, back in their bed.

"You speak from such vast experience," he teased.

"I speak from the standpoint of four orgasms a day, minimum." She playfully bit him on the shoulder.

"Only four?" He eyed her pointedly. "You have had at least five or six a day. I've been counting."

"I said at the minimum."

"Libby, don't let Nathan fall in love with you," he breathed, knowing his words were going to cause her pain.

He felt her little body draw up into a knot.

"What? What do you mean?" she asked so carefully.

"I can see he's getting really attached to you. It's going to hurt him when you leave." Aron didn't analyze his own feelings on the topic. He couldn't afford to.

"What do you want me to do? Be unfriendly?" Emotion was choking her words as they tried to come out of her mouth.

"Well, no." That wasn't what he meant.

"Not cook his favorite foods? I cook all of your

80

favorite foods." Libby was trying desperately to understand. How could she please Aron, if she didn't understand?

"No, that's not what I mean, either." This wasn't easy.

"Do you not want me to help him with his homework?"

"I need you to help him. The rest of us don't always have time to." This wasn't going very well.

"What do you want me to do then, Aron?" Libby was at a loss. Did he want her to leave?

"I don't know, Libby. I just don't want him to get hurt. You're just so easy to love."

She heard his words; she wondered if he realized what he had just said. He was easy to love, also. Libby could have left him in the bed, and returned to Bess's room. His words had hurt her. Badly. She already loved Nathan, and if the truth be known, she was already deeply in love with Aron. Still, lying stiffly, she weighed her options. Leave or stay? Time was so precious and fleeing fast. She decided to stay. Brushing off the hurt from her shoulders like water off a duck's back, she let her muscles relax and fitted her body into his. "I'll remind him often that I'm only temporary. I'll mention my leaving every day. And I'll talk about Bess, and how much he misses her. Does that sound good?"

There was no resentfulness in her voice. He let out an elongated sigh of relief. Libby was so reasonable. "Yeah, Baby. That'll work just fine."

Snuggling down into his body, Libby decided there would be plenty of time to hurt later. For right now, she just wanted to love.

The next day brought trouble. Jacob had promised Libby he would teach her how to ride a horse. Aron had wanted to do it, but he got called away to a meeting with the family lawyers about the management of their parent's trust fund. The economy was hitting everything hard, so it became more of a challenge each year to invest in ventures that provided a decent return. It was also his responsibility to review all the allocations that were meted out to worthy teenagers and sick children. They also had a program to loan out money to cancer patients who wanted to further their education. Necessary business, but Jacob knew Aron hated to be away from Libby and that he would get through the day as quickly as humanly possible.

After listening to Libby plead, Jacob had relented and chosen Molly. She was the most gentle of their horses and he knew Aron would kill him if he let anything happen to Libby. Oh, Aron talked big and pretended that his time with Libby didn't matter to him, but Jacob knew they were falling in love with each other. He also knew that Libby felt like her time was limited, but Jacob was a big believer in positive thinking, faith and miracles.

From his work with the various fund raisers for cancer victims, he knew Doc Mulligan personally and when the Doc had learned that Libby was coming to work at Tebow, he had given Jacob a call himself. The Doc had cautioned Jacob about Libby taking any unnecessary risks. Doctors and science didn't really understand what threw someone who had cancer into remission, or out of it, but there were some studies which suggested that trauma to the body could shorten a remission period. Anyway, there was no use taking chances—that's why he had chosen Molly.

Jacob also knew about the test she had to return for in less than a month. Hopefully, by that time there would be good news and Aron would start coming to his senses. Libby belonged on Tebow. Libby belonged to Aron. Jacob had never been surer of anything.

"Hold the reins like this, Libs. Not too tight." He led the old horse around, adjusting Libby's feet in the stirrups. "That's right. You don't have to be afraid. Molly is as gentle as a lamb."

Libby wasn't afraid; it was just a long way to the ground. Her balance wasn't the best in the world, but this was one thing she had promised herself she would do while she still felt good. "You're doing great, Libby. I'm going to walk you over to the corral and you can just go round and round in a circle until you feel secure enough to take a real jaunt." Jacob's words were reassuring. He wouldn't let anything happen to her, not if he could help it. Smiling, she knew Jacob was fond of her, but he was also scared of Aron.

Aron cared about her. Libby knew that he did. But even if Aron changed his mind about the nature of their relationship, it still wouldn't change the reality of her disease. No, she was in remission, she reminded herself. Remission. She knew the statistics, there was no use playing like she didn't.

"Okay, take off." He set Molly and Libby into a safe little circular path. Or it would have been safe if a big ole chicken snake hadn't decided to crawl across the enclosure. Those old chicken snakes knew no fear. Aron wouldn't let any of them be killed because a) they didn't have any chickens or eggs and b) chicken snakes ate their weight in rats, regularly. Molly didn't know they were harmless, however, and Libby was deathly afraid of even a rubber snake. So when Molly shied from the snake, Jacob hollered, causing Libby to jerk. Molly bucked and Libby trying to hold on - saw the snake, and all hell broke loose. Libby came crashing down. Jacob thought that everything was all right. It was just a little fall. The snake hadn't looked back and Molly didn't step on Libby. But, Libby didn't move. He ran to her and found blood all over the back of her head. She had hit the top railing of the fence on her way down to the ground.

Chapter Five

Aron was homesick. He hadn't even been gone a whole day, but he was nearly aching with longing. And it wasn't Tebow he was homesick for, or his brothers. Aron was homesick for Libby. She had slept in his arms all night, but right now he felt as if a piece of him had been cut off. Never would he have believed that a little slip of a girl could get under his skin the way she had. He thought about her all the time.

Libby had surprised him. She fit into their life like she belonged. Nothing was too much trouble; she pitched in and helped in every project they took on. That is—she tried—Aron had a hard time trying to keep her safe. Other than her overblown fear of snakes, she was absolutely fearless. Just the other day, he had caught her trying to coax one of their biggest Beefmaster bulls into a stall so she could give him a bath. The dignified, registered, blue-blood Warpaint was not amused. Neither was Aron.

Again and again it hit him how different from Sabrina Libby was. He had received a call from their neighbor, Clyde Cummings, an elderly widower. He had requested one of the boys to come over and help him pull a tractor loose that had got stuck in the mud. In the process of trying to free it himself, the old man had hurt his back. Libby had taken Clyde casseroles and soups for a week, until he was feeling up to par. Nothing like that would have ever even occurred to Sabrina. The nice things Libby wanted to do for others reminded Aron of his mother.

The day before yesterday, one of Aron's prize heifers had begun to calve. It was her first, and Aron was worried about her. The bull he had bred her with was big and he didn't want to risk any birth complications. Nothing would do Libby, but to get to attend the blessed event. When Aron had been forced to put his arm up the cow's birth canal and turn the calf, Libby had been right there with hot water and towels. (Not that he needed hot water and towels, but he humored her.) When they finally pulled the little bull free of his mother, Libby had thrown her arms around Aron and almost knocked him down. She had named the little bull Muffin. Now how was that going to look on the official Beefmaster Association Breeder's forms? Actually, Aron didn't care. He was so enamored with Libby that he was almost giddy.

And the sex. Lord Have Mercy, as he always said. The sex was utterly incredible. She was so sweetly responsive, eager and uninhibited—yet, at the same time, enchantingly innocent. It was a heady combination and one that kept him in a state of constant arousal.

Libby had made herself at home at Tebow and, most especially in his heart.

Although the trip had been a necessary one, Aron was glad it was almost over. Never had the road seemed so long from Austin to Kerrville. Never had he been so tempted to floor it. When he got to the last leg of the journey, the dirt road that led from the blacktop to the Tebow ranch gate had never looked so welcoming. He noticed the wildflowers that grew along the way. Had they always been so bright and colorful? Everything seemed better somehow. The air was sweeter, the food tasted better...hell, he even liked his worthless brothers more.

Mostly, he couldn't wait to hold her in his arms again. Last night's loving had only left him hungry for more. That was the way it always was. He just couldn't get enough of Libby Fontaine. Lately, he had been rethinking his future. He had made a decision. A huge decision. He wanted Libby in his life; there was no way he could face a lifetime without her. Marriage wasn't the word he would use just yet, but he was definitely thinking long-term. The only problem was convincing her of that. Something was holding her back. He knew she cared about him. There was no doubt in his mind, since she showed him every day in more ways than he could count.

Why was she so adamant that their time together was short? Yeah, he knew it had been his idea to start with. Hell, he was ready to admit he was wrong. Yet every time he put limits on the relationship, she had been only too happy to agree. Aron didn't like for her to agree so damn readily. He wanted her to fight for him. So, when he got home, the mission had changed. Win Libby Fontaine was his new goal.

When he started up the drive, he knew instantly something was wrong. It was only three o'clock and all of the brother's trucks were there. They were pulled haphazardly around the front, as if they had all been in a hurry to get out and get into the house. His heart clutched in his chest and a wave of anguished concern ripped down his back. The air left his throat, seized in his lungs like wet concrete, and the blood pulsed into his head. He didn't want anything to happen to any of his brothers, but all he could think about was—Oh God—

don't let anything have happened to his precious Libby.

He drove faster as he got closer and ended up skidding his King Ranch dangerously close to the wide front verandah steps. Leaping from the cab, he took the steps three at a time. Charging through the front door, he yelled, "What the hell is wrong? Libby! Libby, answer me right now!"

"We need to call Doc Mulligan." This was Jacob's voice. A doctor? Who was Mulligan? By, God he'd find out. He followed the voices.

"Shit, Aron's here." That was Isaac.

"Like he's not going to find us?" Joseph stage whispered. "We're in the den, Aron!"

Aron barreled into the 'man-cave' as Nathan called it and saw four of his brothers kneeling by the leather sofa. And in front of them was—aw hell, it was his Libby.

In a few short moves, he had displaced brothers both left and right. Kneeling at her side, he whispered, "Libby? Sweetheart?" She was so small and pale and her eyes were closed.

"What the hell happened?" He looked directly at Jacob, pinning him with his menacing gaze.

"Aron, oh Aron." Libby opened her eyes, held out her arms, and as he took her, she began scooting over into his lap. "I am so glad you're here, Aron. So glad. I missed you so."

As Aron cuddled her close, he demanded again. "What happened to her?"

"She fell off of Molly." Jacob's voice was level and quiet.

Aron's hands at once began moving over her body.

Isaac snorted. "It's her head, Aron." Laughing, he said, "I thought I'd tell you before you felt her up in front of us."

"Hush up, Isaac. There's nothing funny about this."

88

Aron's voice was direct and succinct. He held her with one arm, while he began parting her hair, looking for a wound.

"She hit her head on the fence when Molly threw her." Jacob sounded as guilty as he felt.

At Aron's indrawn breath, Libby feared for Molly and Jacob's safety. "It wasn't Jacob's fault, I begged him to teach me. And it wasn't Molly's fault. It was that humongous, horrible deadly snake that scared us!"

Aron fought with everything he had not to smile. This was too serious.

"It was a chicken snake." Jacob muttered dryly.

"A huge, ugly, vicious chicken snake!" Libby was very anti-serpent.

"Why aren't you in the hospital?" He looked at Libby, then at the brothers.

"No, no, no, no." She clung to his neck. "No hospital! Some of the worst days of my life have been spent in hospitals." Aron pulled her closer still, if that was even possible.

Jacob knelt by her and took her hand. Aron's eyes widened. "Libby, see the doctor, please." Jacob's voice was low, but he spoke from his heart.

"I'm fine, Jacob. I don't need to see him." Her eyes pled with him to let it drop. Knowing that Aron would take up Jacob's mantra, Libby changed her tactic. "Aron, please take me to our room. I want to lie down and I need you to hold me."

That's all it took. Aron rose and started off with her. Before he left the room, he turned and faced his brothers. "If I ever come home again and find her with so much as a paper cut, there will be hell to pay. I go off and leave the most precious thing I have in the world in your care and you let a horse throw her," he paused and a small smile escaped his lips, "and a Godzilla-sized snake nearly swallowed her whole. It will not happen again!" With that he stalked off, Libby held close to his heart.

"Yeah, this is a temporary thing. You can tell. He don't care a thing in the world about her." Isaac observed dryly.

***

Throwing back the covers, he carefully laid her down. "Where's your little jammies, baby?" She hadn't worn many sleeping things since the night they became lovers, but he had seen her in sleeping shorts and a tank.

"They're in my suitcase under Bess's bed."

"Baby, why are you still living out of your suitcase?" He put his hands on his hips and looked down at her pointedly.

"I don't stay in that room very much, and this is your room, so the suitcase is more mobile." He looked at her for a moment, and then walked out. Where was he going? Then, it occurred to her – he had gone to Bess's room to hunt her clothes. She held her breath, afraid he would look in the closet and find the pasteboard box that held her most precious treasure. She had purchased Aron's very first sculpture. It was a mustang stallion, head thrown back and mane blowing in the breeze. It was so good that one would think that horse would leap right off of its stand. She didn't know why she was afraid for him to find it – it's not like it would make him angry or anything. Still, a girl had to have some secrets. He didn't need to have his ego grow any bigger than it already was.

In a few seconds, he was back. Relieved he didn't find the box, she saw that he had confiscated her other belongings. He set the suitcase on the bed and took out all of her meager wardrobe. She was embarrassed for him to see how very little she had.

As Aron unpacked for Libby, his throat closed up a little bit when he counted five pairs of panties, two bras, four pairs of jeans and ten tops. This was all she had? Well, he would have to do something about that. He could see a shopping trip in their future. Turning, he emptied two of his drawers, rearranging his things to make room for hers.

"You don't have to do that Aron."

He ignored her argument. Instead, he set about undressing her. Pulling off her top and jeans, he studied her curvy little body. Kneeling by the bed, he unhooked her bra. He kissed each breast, just one time. Next, he pulled her lacy pair of pink panties down her legs and leaned down, kissing the apex of her thighs, right above her small patch of curls. "You scared ten years off my life, Baby. Hold up your arms." Slipping the tank top over her head and the shorts up her legs, he then quickly shucked his clothes, throwing them left and right. "Scoot over." Immediately, he wrapped himself around her, holding her so tight she could barely breathe. "I can't stand the thought of anything happening to you."

"I'm fine. I promise."

"Why was Jacob so insistent that you see a doctor?" Aron carefully enunciated every word, indicating that he expected an answer.

She had no intention of ever lying to him; she would just water down her answer so it was harmless. "I used to have a slight medical condition."

"What kind of medical condition?" Aron rose up, capturing her hands and holding them over her head, effectively immobilizing her. "And I expect a straight answer, Libby."

"It was a blood disorder, but I am perfectly healthy, right now." God, let me be telling him the truth, she prayed.

"A blood disorder...Baby, what does that mean?" Aron began kissing her face, murmuring little endearments against her skin.

"It means I'm fine, I promise." God help her if she was lying. "Aron?" It was time to pull out the big guns. "Aron, can I kiss your winkie?"

A man could swell from an insult, he was proving it. "ELIZABETH, I DO NOT HAVE A WINKIE!"

Libby giggled so hard she snorted. Before she could catch her breath, he was laughing along with her. "Okay, okay. Let me try again. Aron McCoy, sir. May I kiss your Gargantuan Purple Helmeted Warrior?"

"That's more like it, and yes you may." He grinned at her mischievous smile. Then, his blood pressure started to rise. The sexiest woman he had ever been lucky enough to touch had just asked permission to give him a blowjob. "Are you sure you feel like it? You don't have to. I'd be happy just holding you close all night."

"Lose the shorts." She sat up, anxious to get his mind off blood disorders. "Now, you realize I've never actually done this before." All of a sudden she was unsure.

"Anything you do to me will feel incredible. The excitement comes not from the act, but more from who is touching me." He pulled down his shorts, his Johnson was already eight inches long and five inches around, and it wanted whatever Libby wanted to give him. "Where do you want me?" Aron was giving her control.

"I want to sit on the bed and you stand between my legs." He got up off the bed, and turned to face her. She sat in front of him, her luscious hair falling in waves around her shoulders. Spreading her legs, she held out her hand. "Come to me, Baby."

Excitement was making his toes curl. "You know I won't last long this way."

"You won't have to, Aron. This is going to excite me as much as it will you." He stood still, fully at her mercy. Taking a deep breath, she eyed her prey. "My mouth is watering just looking at you, Aron. My lands, you are beautiful." Her first move surprised him. Instead of going right for his dick, she cradled his balls. Gently massaging them, she tested their weight.

"Ohhh, Little One, you have talented hands." Closing his eyes, he pushed his hips toward her, begging for more. She didn't let him down. Libby took his penis in her hands, as if she were about to say a prayer, her palms flat, fingers meeting at the base. Pulling him close, she kissed it gently, putting her mouth over the head. Aron jerked in her hands. Using the tips of her fingers, she began to massage him, putting one fist over the other she twisted up and over Aron's cock, touching the tip of her tongue to the little open slit every time it was exposed. Soon Aron was shaking, just waiting for the gentle, wet touch. His hips began to buck, so she gave in to what she wanted. Slipping her lips over the top, she opened her throat and accepted as much of him into her mouth as she could. "God, Libby. I thought you said you've never done this before." It was difficult for Libby to be still, so she just matched the movement of her hips with her mouth. "Suck me, suck me, Libby." Tightening her lips, she provided as much suction and heat as she could. "Oh, yeah, that's it. You're so good," he praised her.

Letting go with her hands, she accepted another half inch down her throat and drew him closer. She kneaded his tight butt, loving the feel of all that incredible muscle. Emotion welled up in her heart and she groaned her pleasure. The vibration of her throat caused Aron to buck forward. Removing her hands from his hips, she grabbed his fingers and moved them to the back of her head. Slipping her mouth off for the slightest second, she requested, "You take control."

It was music to his ears. She was wet, tight, hot and exciting as all get out. Twisting her hair around one hand, he held her at his mercy. Aron was so excited that it was hard to be careful, but he refused to hurt her. Still, her mouth was absolute heaven and getting to pump into her at will was beyond compare. His dick swelled to almost bursting, his blood ringing in his ears. Her mouth was so sweet. Her little tongue was never still; it put as much pressure on him as her lips did. A frantic frenzy took over. He held her face still and pumped deep. Angling her head, he nudged his length down her throat. Bless her heart, she didn't gag even once. She opened herself up to him and provided him a place to play. Swallowing, she heightened his pleasure ten-fold. He would bet his life this was pure instinct on her part. But God, she had no idea how it made him feel. "Swallow again, Precious. That was wild." She did as he asked. Suddenly, she made her lips impossibly tight, sending him over the edge. "Damn! Baby! Do you want me to pull out or can you take it?" He was asking if she would swallow. He waited for a sign from her. Gritting his teeth, he held back until she clasped his hips again, holding him in place, letting him know she intended to accept his release into her mouth. "Lord Have Mercy," he mumbled. She was relentless, bearing down with the sweetest tension. Bellowing aloud, he shot his essence down her throat and she accepted it like she was born to it.

Afterward, she was reluctant to let him go, moving her tongue against him even in his spent state. Bending over, he took her face in his hands and as he pulled out of her mouth, he placed his lips over hers, showing her how grateful he was for the gift she had given him.

Pushing her back, he followed her over. "You are

94

perfection, did you know that?" Rolling to her side, she snuggled up to him.

"I did pretty well for my first time, huh?" She nudged her face against him, petting him like a contented cat.

"There is no one like you, Libby. No one even comes close."

Moving against him again, he realized she was in need. "What do you want, Doll? I'll do anything, all you have to do is ask."

"Will you put your knee up against me, between my legs, and let me ride? I've fantasized about doing that." Just hearing the words come out of her mouth made his cock twitch back to life.

"Gladly, Doll. Pleasing you is the greatest pleasure I could ever have." He positioned himself to accommodate her request, pressing his knee between her thighs.

"Wait, Aron. I'm already wet. Let me change and put on something clean. You don't want to get my stuff all over your leg." She got up off the bed and went to dig in the drawer where he put her underwear. His mouth dropped. Was she serious?

"Come back here, Libby." She stopped to see what was wrong. "Pull off your panties, Baby. I want to feel all of you—wet and wild—right against my skin. Feeling how excited you are is like a badge of honor for me; it's my way of knowing I'm doing something right." He held his hand out to her.

"Are you sure?" She was serious.

"Honey, if you leave your sweet cream on my thigh, all it'll do is please the hell out of me." Flashing him a little smile, she hung her thumbs in the waist band of her sleep shorts and pulled down, revealing his private treasure. Already he was swelling, but first he

95

would give her what she asked for and then he'd give her what she needed. Taking her by the waist he lifted her, and as she came over him, he set her down on his thick thigh, fitting the hard muscle right against her swollen center.

"Aron, that feels so good." He bent his leg and let her mold her body to his. Wrapping both her legs around one of his, she held on for dear life and began to pull her clitoris back and forth over his hair-roughened thigh. Laying her head on his shoulder, she let herself go.

Aron was absolutely enchanted. He'd never seen anything so erotic in his life. Her mouth-watering, heart-shaped bottom was bobbing up and down and her incredible breasts were scrubbing up and down on his chest revving his engines to the highest gear. Unable to stop himself, he plucked at her nipples, causing her to moan. She humped his leg and honest to God he thought he would die. "Libby, you are a fuckin' miracle."

With glazed eyes, she looked at him – she was in a frenzy. "This is wonderful, Aron – but please tell me you're hard. I need you so badly I could cry."

With a triumphant shout, he picked her up and moved her down to his cock which was standing up straight – ready, willing and able. "Take me, Libby. Rise up and let me in."

Heated and aroused, she reached between her legs and closed her fist around his fully engorged cock. Holding steady, she eased down, taking him inside of her. "Oh, God, Aron. You are so big. You fill me up so good." Libby shivered with absolute delight as she lowered herself fully until she was completely impaled.

Aron sighed. There was no greater pleasure in the world than working his way into her warm welcoming pussy, savoring the feel of her taut inner muscles parting just for him. "You've been wanting to take a ride—now's your chance. Give me your hands, Sweetheart."

96

She did, her eyes wide with excitement, their radiant flames warming him deep inside.

"I don't know how to move, you've got to help me." Before when they made love, Aron was always in control. Now that she had the reins, she wanted to do it right.

"My pleasure, Doll, my pleasure." Aron was so ready to rock and roll, that it took every ounce of control he had to take his time with her. This was about Libby, damn it. "You don't have to bounce up and down. It feels better for both of us if you rock gently back and forth to begin with." He felt her move, Holy Mother of God, she was sweet, like pure warm liquid velvet. "Yeah, just like that. See Baby, you wanted to ride something, now you are. You're too precious to risk on a real horse, so I'll just let you ride my rocking horse."

If it hadn't felt so good, she would've laughed at him, but her clit was having a party on his pelvic bone as she rode herself to heaven and back. Before long, she sped up, her intimate strokes settling into a perfectly delicious pace.

Her breasts were bouncing sweetly and his hands couldn't stay away. Aron decided to offer his support, so he cupped her tits, massaging her sensitive rosy nipples as she gyrated and undulated on his stiff cock. Libby dug her nails into his thigh in reaction.

For a while, he let her have her fun. If he wasn't about to explode – he could have watched her rapturous expression all day. Soon, however, it began to get serious for him. He was going to cum, regardless. Wanting Libby to finish first, he decided to help out a little. She made it easy. All he had to do was swirl his fingers around her clit and tell her what he wanted. She was so in tune to him, it was scary. "I need you to come, Doll. You've driven me mad with desire and I can't hold out much longer. And I refuse to come before my Libby finds her pleasure." That he was able to have a semi-coherent conversation was a miracle. Before he could get his explanation finished, the tiny contractions began. "That's my girl! Ah, Libby, you are a goddess." She put her hands on his rippled stomach and ground down on him. Her pussy gripped his cock, gripped it and squeezed like a fist. Letting go, he clutched her by the hips and lifted her whole body a couple of inches in the air. Aron drove into her with thrusting, staccato like strokes. "Yes! Yes!" he shouted, his own climax overtaking him. Every neuron in his spinal column sizzled with satisfaction.

Libby watched him come, the pleasure manifesting itself on his face. He was a beautiful sight, arching his back, forcing that mile-wide chest up so she could caress and knead it as he convulsed beneath her. His cock was shooting ropes of cum deep within her. She wanted to memorize every sensation, every feeling, every thought. His muscles strained, his neck bowed, his eyes shut, God, he even began to whisper her name in a prayer like litany. It was just too much. "Aron! It's starting again, I just came and now – oh Lord – I'm coming again."

In his mindless euphoria, he was aware she held her own breasts, pulling at the nipples, doubling her pleasure, prolonging the joy. Overwhelmed, he sat up and pulled her close, shaking with the sweetest release he had ever experienced.

Libby held his head, wiped the sweat from his brow, pushed his hair back and kissed him right between the eyes. "There is no one like you. What did I ever do to deserve the gift of these precious days with you? Until my dying day, I will treasure every second I've spent in your arms." Hugging him close, she caressed him until he calmed.

"Libby, you've taken me by surprise. I never expected to find anyone like you." Reverently, he framed her face and touched their lips together in a tender kiss. He lay back, pulling her down with him. Still intimately joined, she lay on his chest, mindlessly rubbing her fingers over his upper arm. Aron wanted to say more, but when he looked down – his baby was fast asleep.

The next morning Libby said she felt as good as new. She was still getting up at least an hour before everybody else and they were all becoming fat and happy from her exquisite cooking. Aron had woken up with a whole host of things he wanted to do. Primarily, he intended to learn as much about Miss Fontaine as possible. He was going to escort her out on the town and take her camping. In Aron's own cowboy way, he planned on wooing Libby.

***

Libby was worried to death. Something was wrong...Aron had changed. As she put together Nathan's brown bag lunch, she weighed her options. What she wanted, she couldn't have. She wanted Aron. She wanted a future. Libby wanted to live on Tebow and get pregnant with Aron's babies. Libby wanted to live.

Okay, so she hadn't been given a death sentence. After all, she was in remission. In three weeks she would have a check-up, and if all still looked good, well then—who was to say that she wouldn't live to be eighty? Holding on to the cabinet door, she pinched the wood so tightly she wouldn't have been surprised to find marks left from her fingers.

"Libby?" It was Nathan. "Do you have some lunch for me?"

Behind Nathan came Aron and Jacob. They were headed to a cattle auction. Aron had asked her to go along, but she had promised herself that today would be the day she made a detailed grocery list. The pantry and freezer were beginning to need refilling. Next, she would have to find out the logistics of how she would get there and how to pay for the food. It hurt Libby to have to ask those questions; she wished more than anything that these men were her family, and that taking care of them was more than just her job.

Seeing Aron reminded Libby that she needed to talk to Nathan at the first opportunity and remind him of her temporary status. Handing Nathan his lunch, she answered, "I sure do, Big Man. Ham and cheese sandwiches, apple chips and lemon bars. Does that sound like something you'd like?" Nathan stepped forward and clasped her around the waist.

"Thanks Libs." He had heard Aron call her that. "And thanks for helping me with the paper last night. You are really smart. I didn't know there were so many different Indian tribes living in Texas so long ago. And that program saved my life, it made everything a lot easier. I don't know what we ever did before you came along."

Returning his hug, she looked guiltily at the men watching her. Why did she feel like she was doing something wrong? Trying to do as Aron asked, she cleared her throat and began. "You did just fine before I came. Miss Bess took great care of you and when I'm gone, she'll be right here taking good care of you again. You know I don't want to leave, but I have to. This is your home and Bess's. I'm just merely passing through." Patting Nathan on the back, she looked up at Aron with a small smile and an expectant look, seeking his approval. She was trying to do as he asked.

Aron excused himself from his brother and

whacked Nathan on the shoulder as he left to catch the bus. His baby was looking at him with the saddest eyes. He knew she was just doing as he had asked; she was trying to remind Nathan that her time at Tebow would soon draw to a close.

Well, to hell with that!

He should never have asked her to distance herself from any of them. He was a fool, and it was time this fool set things straight. She had turned away from him and was watching Nathan walk toward the road. He slipped up behind her and caught her back against him. She melted into him like butter on toast.

"Did I please you?"

Turning her in his arms, he pushed her back and back until he had her cornered in the butler's pantry. "You have pleased me in countless ways, Libby: the heat of your kisses pleases me, the feel of your pebbled nipple on my tongue pleases me, and the grip of your pussy around my aching cock pleases me. I'd say everything about you pleases the hell out of me." He held her flat against the wall, both of her hands captive in one of his. Touching his forehead to hers, he pinned her down. "But, I find that what you did this morning, telling Nathan we would get along just fine without you – that pleased me not at all." Aron growled out the last words.

Straining to read his expression, Libby was confused. "I did as you asked, Aron. I reminded Nathan I was leaving, and that Bess would be back where she belonged."

"I know you did as I asked, but you didn't take one thing into consideration." He began to rain peppery little kisses all over her face, attempting to convey to her how much he cherished her.

"What's that?" He had magical kisses. Libby

arched her neck, giving him full access to her neck, and when he dipped down to the open vee of her T-shirt, she shamelessly thrust her breasts against him, begging for him to take his petting to the next level.

Aron laid his head on her shoulder, allowing her to lower her hands, and she immediately settled them around his waist. He said nothing for a few moments, and then he spoke softly, "You didn't take into consideration that I am a fool, I can't stand the thought of you leaving. Sweetheart, I don't ever want you to leave." Dropping to his knees, he nudged her shirt up with his nose and he kissed her soft, flat belly.

Libby was shaking. Cradling his head in her hands, she turned his face up to look at her. "Aron, it's okay. I know Bess is coming back, and I know there's no legitimate place for me here."

"You're wrong. There is a place for you here. In my home, in my room, in my bed, but most importantly...in my heart." Damn! He was about to make a declaration in the crappin pantry. Without asking, he picked her up and headed for the stairs.

"Aron, it's not even eight o'clock. We just got up, and you have to leave for an auction in less than an hour." Not that she was complaining, she would never, ever turn down a chance to love on Aron.

"I realize that, but I forgot to do something last night." Thank goodness his door was open, he didn't want to slow down long enough to open it, but he did kick it closed. "I can work wonders in an hour."

"Yes, you can," she agreed with him. "You are a master of the erotic experience, a connoisseur of caresses, an oracle of orgasms..." Aron tackled her and for a few wonderful moments, they wrestled around on the bed. "It's not fair..." Libby gasped.

Aron straddled her, holding her immobile. "What's not fair?" he queried, smiling like the devil he was.

102

"You're so much bigger than me, I don't have a chance." Her mouth puckered into a pout, which he kissed away.

"You like me bigger," he teased, his eyes alight with mischief, rubbing his groin against her privates.

"Well, true." He had her full attention. Lord, he was an irresistible force.

Aron sobered, climbing off and stretching out beside her. "You like me bigger, because I can take care of you."

She stared into his eyes; they were the color of a summer storm. "I've enjoyed that sensation, yes." She couldn't bring herself to say the words which would lay claim to him. She didn't have any right to expect his care. She was temporary.

"Let me take care of you now, Libby." Slowly he undressed her, kissing each exposed area tenderly before moving on. Next, he shed his own clothing. No words were necessary. He knew she wanted the same thing he did.

Sitting up on the edge of the bed, he pulled her into his lap. He placed her smooth back to his front. Libby nestled into his lap snuggly, with a wiggle. His organ was distended to such a degree, that when she opened her legs, he slid right in between them, not entering her, but cradled securely within the folds of her labia so that her clitoris was riding high on the head of his cock. She could look between her legs and see the weeping tip. "This feels good."

She reached down and caressed him and he groaned. "Hold on, don't get ahead of me here. You know how you affect me." Opening the drawer of his nightstand he took out a little vial of oil.

"What's that?" Curiosity got the best of her.

"Massage oil," his voice was husky with desire.

"What are you going to massage?"

"You."

"Oh." Her breath hitched in response.

He rubbed the oil on his hands. A little earthquake of excitement shivered up her spine. He felt the tremble, and he chuckled, knowing she was dying of anticipation.

"I smell chocolate."

"Mmmmmmm, love chocolate, it's my favorite flavor." He licked the side of her neck and she quivered. "No, I take that back—it used to be my favorite flavor. Now it's number two." Nipping her shoulder blade, he clarified, "You're my number one flavor. But to be specific, the scent I'm about to massage into your soft skin is Chocolate Crème Brule."

"Sounds yummy." Actually, it did. Several places on her body were calling for a taste.

He rubbed the oil into his hands and she practically shouted hallelujah when he cupped her breasts. From this angle all she could do was lay back and enjoy. Dang! There were so many things to enjoy; she decided to count the ways. One, his chest felt glorious against her back as she slowly moved from left to right and back again. Two, those talented hands were shaping and kneading her breasts as if they were molding clay and he was creating a masterpiece. Third, her vagina was opening like a night blooming flower, aching to be claimed and filled. "Aron, it's too much."

"No, it's not." He proceeded to love her from head to toe. Sinking his teeth into her neck, he held her still like a stallion would a mare. With his forefingers, he traced circles around her nipples – wide, concentric circles that shrunk with each lap.

"Please, please." she begged. If he didn't touch her nipples, she thought she just might scream. The warmth of his hands and her body combined to heat the
104

fragrance so that the chocolate smelled like hot fudge. "Nipples, Aron, please pinch my nipples,"

"My Libby's a little Wild-woman," he growled approvingly. He rewarded her boldness. Taking both nipples between his fingers, he rolled them, arousing her to frantic heights. Twisting her head back, she blindly sought his lips. Aron feasted at her mouth, sucking on her tongue, as he manipulated her breasts into trembling mounds of passion. Her cream was anointing his cock, proclaiming a desperate need for his brand of possession.

In a fever-pitch, she was totally uninhibited, abandoning all pretense of propriety. "I've got to have you, Aron. Please, come inside me – I'm so empty." She raised her hips in supplication. "Take me, Sweetheart, don't make me wait. I need you so." Libby was pleading, begging for his love.

Aron lifted her, his hardness seeking her heat like a moth to a flame. She opened to him, her vulva swollen and flushed to a deep rose. With a moan of relief, her body stretched to receive the full length and breadth of his pulsating staff. Almost immediately she flew apart, he literally had to hold on tight to keep her from catapulting out of his arms. She shook, her body shuddering with intense spasms. Aron was amazed at her ability to give herself over to him, taking whatever he offered and giving him more than he ever dreamed he could demand. "That's my good girl. That's my baby."

Her unmitigated enthusiasm was a powerful aphrodisiac. Aron became a mad man, his hips pistoning in and out of her like an out of control jack-hammer. Laying back, flat on the bed, he pulled Libby back with him. "Stay with me, Cowgirl," he encouraged as he bent his knees to give her body something to push down against. Using her breasts as the world's most glorious hand-holds, he moved her up and down on his shaft, her whole body sliding up and down the full length of his torso. Wrapping a leg over each of his, she moved in tandem with him until he bellowed his fulfillment. Shivers and jerks of pure pleasure made her whole body quiver in response to his powerful climax. They lay quietly for a time, until he coaxed her to turn over on top of him. There was something he had to say, and there was no better time than the present. "Libby, look at me."

She was wonderfully sated, but lifted her eyes to meet his. Unable to resist, she shifted upward to place her lips softly on his. One sweet heartbeat later, she whispered, "You have made me so happy, Aron."

"Libby," he began, but she interrupted him.

"Aron, I want to have a few adventures. Would it make you mad if Joseph taught me how to sky dive?"

Chapter Six

"What?" he yelled so loud, he almost knocked her out of bed. He had been about to proclaim his undying love and she was thinking of ways to kill herself.

"He assures me it will be perfectly safe." She was biting that lower lip with those little pearly white teeth and looking like she was anticipating an ice cream cone.

"Libby..."

"And, I know you nixed the idea at first, but tonight—I'd really like to ride Isaac's motorcycle with him to the pool hall. He's going to teach me how to play snooker." She was lying right on top of him, her chin held up in her hands, her eyes wide open and twinkling. If she had asked him for the deed to Tebow right then, he would have signed it over. God, what he wouldn't do for her.

"Why are you so determined to live like there's no tomorrow?"

His innocent question ripped a hole in Libby's heart.

"None of us are promised tomorrow, Aron. I want to live today, just in case there is no tomorrow. But, rest assured. All of this other stuff is just fluff. I want to do it, don't get me wrong. I have a battle to fight and an enemy to face, so I want to enjoy my life now—today." Taking his face in her hands, she held him still, so there was no chance he could miss what she had to say. "But, what you have given me—the gift of you—puts the rest of it to shame." With one last smacking kiss, she jumped up and started to hurriedly redress. He lay there, sort of dumb struck. What had happened? He had been about to declare his unending devotion and now the love of his life was off to bar-hop and throw herself out of an airplane.

"Libby, I nearly had an apoplectic fit when you took a baby spill off a fourteen year old nag."

She didn't do it often, so she didn't do it well, but what the hay! Libby proceeded to pout. Her bottom lip snuck out from her top lip, just a tiny fraction, and she made her eyes round and sad.

It didn't take much...he couldn't stand it. "Come here." He held out his arms. The fact that he was still outstandingly naked, just added to the hug appeal. She bounded across the room to him. Catching her, he held her close.

"I'll be careful, I promise."

"I have conditions." He rubbed her back, wishing he could tie her to the bed and keep her there. That flash of fantasy almost made him forget what he was about to say. Libby...tied to a bed...

"What conditions?" She didn't sound resentful at all. In fact, she sounded pleased that he cared enough to demand them. She spoke from the comfort of his lap, her head resting on his wide shoulder.

"You jump attached to Joseph." He was serious about that part. "And I wait at the landing spot with a truck load of mattresses."

He felt her body vibrate with giggles against his chest. "What else?"

"You can ride Isaac's motorcycle if you wear a helmet, and if he doesn't drive any faster than thirty-five miles an hour." Her little fist tapped him lightly on the chest.

"Okay, forty-five." Hey, he was being generous here.

"Any more?"

"Yes, he can teach you to play snooker. But no tequila shots and I will come and check on you at some point in the evening."

Big sigh. "All right, Mother." Frankly, it felt fabulous to be cherished. God, how she would enjoy a lifetime of his brand of loving.

Something large and hard poked her in the thigh. "I am not your mother."

"No kidding."

***

Aron tried to put the pieces together. He had a Herculean task on his hands. Winning the hand of the exquisite Libby Fontaine was going to require dedication and concentration.

Something was not right. Aron decided he would corner her and make her talk about herself. No, he had to be more subtle than that.

"Do you like that bull?" Jacob pointed to the spotted longhorn standing on the auction block, ready to be bought by the highest bidder.

Shit! He had lost track of where he was, much less what was for sale. "What do you think?" Aron put the monkey back on his brother's back.

"You're not paying a bit of attention are you?" Jacob knew Aron.

"No, I'm worrying about Libby." He really was. She was hiding something monumental from him, and he didn't know why.

"What about Libby?" He forgot to hide the concern in his voice. Aron picked up on it right away.

"You know something, don't you, you scoundrel?" Why was it that Jacob was closer in some ways to his lover than he was?

"What I know, I can't tell." At least Jacob was honest. And hard-headed.

"If you keep information from me, and I end up losing her—I'll never forgive you." Aron laid his cards on the table.

Jacob let out a tortured breath. "Let me think about it."

"Don't wait too long." Aron admonished him.

"You're a smart guy," Jacob encouraged him. "See if you can figure it out."

While Jacob bought and sold cattle, Aron tried to put two and two together. It bothered him how little he knew about Libby. To know her body so intimately, he knew very little about her life. One thing was for certain, he intended to rectify the situation.

Going back to the day she fell off the horse, he remembered Jacob saying the name of a doctor. What was it? Montgomery? No. Monroe? No. Mulligan, yeah. Mulligan. He took a pen out of his pocket and wrote the name on the back of his auction program. He saw Jacob take note of his remembrance.

What else? Oh, her innocence—Libby had said that she hadn't had a normal life up to this point. Something about a family problem. Whatever it was, it had kept her from interacting with men to any degree. He hated to think about her having problems, but he couldn't regret that he had been the sole recipient of all the incredible passion Libby had stored up.

Third, she'd said she was going to have to fight a battle and face an enemy. Damn! That didn't sound good. Aron wondered if she was in some type of trouble. Didn't she know that he'd move heaven and earth to help her? Not that he had told her in so many words, but right now, she didn't act like she wanted to hear any talk of forever. And forever was exactly what Aron wanted to nail down.

"Are you ready to go?" Aron looked up and the auction was over. Crap! He had missed it all.

"Yeah, I guess so. Did we do good?" Actually, he didn't really care a whole hell of a lot—one way or the other.

"Excellent. How about you, got a handle on Libby, yet?"

"Hell, no." But, he was working on it.

"Keep plugging at it, you'll figure it out."

***

It was hard to stand by and watch Libby ride off on the back of Isaac's hog. He had insisted she wear a helmet and reminded her that he would be dropping into Shorty's at some point during the evening. Standing until he couldn't see the dust from the motorcycle, he slowly turned to walk back to the now empty feeling house. With a heavy heart, he realized this was just a small taste of how it would be if Libby were really gone. Not going to happen—he promised himself that. A step or two later, his cell phone rang. It was Trahan, the PI he called upon from time to time about various things.

"McCoy."

"Aron, I have a small lead on the buyer of that bronze you've been trying to track down."

"Tell me." He still wanted to know, but oddly, it wasn't as high of a priority as it used to be.

"The other artist who was exhibiting with you at the time was a woman. I think her name was Martinez. Anyway, I found her and I questioned her about that day, and she recalled the woman who bought

'Freedom'.

"A woman? That's not much to go on."

"The reason it sticks out in Martinez' mind was that she had seen the buyer before. She didn't recall a name, but she does remember a story on the news about the woman having had cancer and there was a benefit of some kind for her medical bills."

"So, this woman spent hard earned money that people donated to her on a bronze when she didn't have enough to pay her doctor and hospital bills?"

"Doesn't sound right, does it?"

"No, it doesn't. I guess it's a start, but I don't know how I can use the information."

"Thought you'd want to know."

"Thanks."

***

Libby was fascinated by the pool hall. She hadn't dressed up, since she didn't have anything to dress up in. But, she was definitely having a good time. The music was loud and very country. Several cowboys had asked her to dance, and she had taken two up on it. Both times, either Isaac or Jacob had cut in when they felt the man was taking liberties. She hadn't felt threatened at any time, but she appreciated the McCoy brothers' concern. It wasn't like they were cramping her style. Libby wasn't there to find a man—she had one. At least, she was claiming him. Not that they were dating or anything. He had never said anything about taking her anywhere. Still, she would rather be with him—anywhere—than with anyone else in the world.

Still and all, like her mom used to say, this place was far better than she had expected. She was here for the experience, and so far, she wasn't disappointed.

Aron could have brought her, but she knew he

112

would have positioned her at his side and under his arm all night and she wouldn't have gotten a taste for the true atmosphere of the place. With the other two McCoys along, Libby could go out on a limb and not fear falling off.

The billiards game was a blast. Isaac taught her how to hold a cue stick and how to rack up the balls. He had even held her close while she learned the proper way to make a shot. There had been no flirting; all the brothers treated her with great care and the utmost respect. They knew who she belonged to – at least for now.

Aron had put his foot down about the tequila shots, so Libby had opted for wine coolers instead. They were really, really, really good. This was her first venture into the world of adult beverages. Every time Jacob and Isaac walked off, Libby ordered another. She hoped they brought enough money to pay her bar tab. She should have felt bad, but right now—actually—she was feeling pretty good.

There were about a dozen men in the place who couldn't keep their eyes off of her. They watched her sway and twirl, right by herself. She had no idea how sexy she was, or that Isaac and Jacob had walked around and informed all of the drooling men she was off limits. They made it clear she was Tebow property, belonging to the big man himself, Aron McCoy. No, Libby didn't have a clue. She was in her own little world. Dancing right by herself, minding her own business. With her wine coolers.

Isaac who was on Libby-patrol, had to take a bathroom break. And while he was gone a group of new men came in. When Jacob noticed, there were several wranglers circling her like Mako sharks. He swooped in and gathered her close. "How many of those drinks have you had, Cutie?"

"Eight." Libby answered with an absolutely straight face.

"Eight!" Jacob exclaimed. "Shorty, why in the hell did you let her have eight wine coolers?" He shouted across the bar.

Shorty grinned, but yelled back. "There's not much alcohol in a wine cooler."

"There is when you've had eight of 'em," he grumbled under his breath. Hell! Aron was going to kill them all.

"Hello, Lover." A sultry voice purred next to Jacob's ear. "Care to introduce me to your tipsy little friend?" Venom dripped off every word.

Jacob's stomach turned over as he recognized Aron's ex-wife's voice—Sabrina. If he hated anybody in the world, it was this woman. "I was never your lover, Bitch." Jacob bit the words out at her. He hadn't forgiven her, nor would he—ever.

His attitude sobered Libby to a degree. "Jacob?" she called his name in confusion.

"It's okay, Libby. This is nobody you need to be concerned with." He held her protectively to his side, as if Sabrina was a disease that would rub off on her.

"She'd best be concerned." Sabrina draped a skinny arm around Jacob's neck. She was over-made up, under dressed, and her perfume had been applied with a heavy hand. "I didn't have my fill of you. She just might have reason to be jealous."

Sabrina's tongue might be dripping sugar, but her eyes were like poisonous darts. These McCoy men owed her—big time. She had been cheated out of a fortune.

"I'm not with Jacob," Libby informed her. "I'm with Aron." Jacob was surprised Libby would publicly claim Aron. He glared at her, pleasantly surprised.

"Interesting!" the woman exclaimed. "Jacob, does

she know who I am?"

"Who are you?" Libby asked, just drunk enough to care.

"I'm Sabrina McCoy, Aron's wife."

The smooth answer made Libby's skin crawl. Her eyes narrowed. "No, you're not. You're divorced. You weren't a good wife." Libby repeated things well.

"Aron wasn't much of a husband. And being his wife wasn't much of a life."

Her flip answer made Libby's blood boil. "Anyone lucky enough to be married to Aron McCoy should get down on their hands and knees and thank the Lord for their blessings." This was a long speech for an inebriated woman.

"The only blessing about living at Tebow was the smorgasbord of gorgeous McCoy men to sample. Jacob here, was one tasty morsel." She leered at Jacob. About that time Isaac walked up. "And here's the tastiest one of them all." Isaac looked grim, and his mouth was twisted as if he had bit into something bitter.

"You didn't sleep with Aron's brothers." Libby was furious, her beautiful features filled with anger.

"I didn't?" Sabrina teased Libby. "And how would you know?"

"I know them. And they wouldn't betray their brother that way." She was emphatic in her support of the McCoy brothers.

"Where is your lover, if that is what he is? And why are you here with Jacob and Isaac if you belong to Aron? Are you following in my footsteps, Sweetie?"

The woman was beautiful. Libby could see why Aron would have been attracted to her. And she was dressed to kill. Libby felt plain and out of place next to her. "That's none of your business," Libby flared. "But I can promise you that Aron's brothers treat me with the greatest respect."

"How about the younger one? Nathan, was it? Is he still as much of a stupid retard as he used to be? Wasn't he born that way? Was it a birth complication or something?" Sabrina stood there looking smug while she lambasted every member of the family that Libby loved so well.

"He has dyslexia, you baboon. I've heard enough from you! That's it." Libby handed her wine cooler to Isaac. "You're going down, you loud-mouthed Jezebel!" Without warning, Libby propelled herself right on top of Sabrina Jones—ex-McCoy. Before Sabrina could get her bearings, Libby had knocked her into a table filled with glasses and beer. Then into another table. Crashes of glass and gasps of amusement echoed through the bar. And it wasn't over.

"Catfight!"

Libby would not give up. Every time Sabrina would try and get away, Libby would get right in her face again. Isaac held Jacob back, both of them fascinated at the little thing's determination. When she picked up a chair to bash over Sabrina's head, Jacob's common sense finally won out and he intervened. Shorty was not happy. He was on the phone and naming names. Jacob held Libby off the ground while she kicked and wiggled to get down and back into the fight. "If I ever see you anywhere near a member of the McCoy family again, I'll take you apart with my bare hands. I'll rip your hair to smithereens. I'll break both your knee caps and stomp your toes…" The threats trailed off as Libby was carted out of the bar to ensure the safety of the clientele. Isaac followed at a safe distance.

Isaac was troubled to see that Sabrina had landed a blow or two. There were bruises and scrapes on Libby's arms and a dark, fist-shaped mark was starting to show on her left jaw.

"You have got to come and get them, Deputy; I'm tired of these McCoys tearing up my place." Shorty called on his cell phone.

"Shit, Jacob. We're about to get arrested," Isaac whispered. He couldn't afford to spend any more time in jail.

"Actually, I think Libby is the one in trouble," Jacob observed—which was worse, much worse.

"With the law. That's nothing. We're the ones up shit creek without a paddle. We have to face Aron."

Isaac was right—and that was a scary proposition.

***

Libby had never seen the inside of a jail. It was as fascinating as the bar had been. This was a new experience she hadn't counted on. She had question after question and soon all the deputies all had pained looks on their faces. Jacob and Isaac sat to one side, their hats in their hands, and waited for one very large Texas tornado to blow in.

"Isaac, I thought I told you that if you got into another bar fight I'd take the cost of the damages out of your hide." Aron stormed into the sheriff's office, growling like an angry bear.

"It wasn't Isaac, Mr. McCoy." A friendly little Barney Fife type approached Aron with a clip board in his hand.

"Jacob? Well, hell this is his first offense; you ought to let him off."

"The problem wasn't just the damage, Mr. McCoy. It was the terroristic-type threats," the deputy cheerfully explained.

"Jacob was making terroristic threats? Against who?" Aron couldn't believe this. He was probably defending Libby's honor. If anybody had touched his baby, they wouldn't live to see another day.

"It wasn't Jacob making the terroristic threats, Mr. McCoy, nor Isaac."

"Well, then you have the wrong people in custody. There were no other members of my family there to cause trouble," Aron roared.

"It was Libby," Isaac muttered low enough that he thought maybe Aron wouldn't hear.

He heard.

"What did you say?" Aron was pole-axed.

"Libby was the one in the fight. She was the one making threats." Isaac lowered his head and winced as if anticipating a blow.

"My Libby isn't capable of doing those things." Aron had no doubt about the truth of his statement.

"It's true, Mr. McCoy." About that time Sheriff Foster joined them.

"Who in the hell did she fight with or threaten?" Aron still didn't believe a word they were saying. And just where in the hell was she? He looked around. She wasn't anywhere in sight.

"She attacked and made threats against one, Sabrina McCoy." The Sheriff looked perplexed, as if he had just made the connection. "Does that name ring a bell with you, Sir?"

"Shit. Yes." It was all beginning to make sense now.

"Where is Libby?" He looked around at all the people who had failed him.

"She's back in the holding cell."

"THE HOLDING CELL? YOU PUT THAT SWEET LIITLE GIRL IN A CELL?" The walls of the jail began to vibrate.

When he bellowed, Libby heard him.

"Aron! Aron! Sweetie, I'm back here! Come meet

these nice criminals."

***

There was a whole herd of Texas longhorns stampeding through Libby's head. "I'm never taking another sip of alcohol as long as I live." It was Saturday and the boys had decided to take a rare day off from any and all duties. Mainly, because Aron insisted. Libby needed him. He was in the man cave, on the middle cushion of the big leather couch and she was literally draped across his lap. Her head lay on the left cushion, her feet were on the right and her middle was cradled across Aron's thighs so he could rub her back.

"A sip wouldn't have hurt anything, Baby. It was the ninety-six ounces that brought you down." He would never tell her, but her soused was the cutest thing he had ever seen.

"I'm so sorry, Aron. I've caused tongues to wag." Her voice was muffled in the material of the couch.

"Don't you worry about it; you're my champion." She bounced a little, and then groaned. He smiled. And he wasn't kidding—he would have given anything to see her lay in on Sabrina. Libby cared. There was no doubt about that...this was proof positive.

"Don't make me laugh, it causes me great pain."

He pushed her shirt up so he could enjoy the silk of her skin as he continued his petting. "I want you to think about something while you're recuperating. A pattern is beginning to emerge in your escapades." He waited for her to grunt before he continued. "On your first adventure you fell off Molly."

Her garbled response made him smile.

"I know it was the snake's fault, but still you got hurt." He began to draw pictures on her back, and then they turned into words. "Second, you wanted to learn to shoot pool and you got involved in a bar-fight, which I appreciate, by the way. Like I said, you're my champion. Sabrina needed to be brought down a notch, and we couldn't do it. The thing I hate is that you got hurt once more. Cuts, scrapes and a big ole' bruise that hurts my heart."

"I'm okay. I just can't believe I've spent time in jail. How am I ever going to live down my unfortunate incarceration?" Was she crazy? Aron was writing on her back, and if she kept real still—maybe she could tell what he was writing.

"Libby, I had you out of that cell ten minutes after I arrived. Your total time-served was only an hour and a half." He kept writing and she kept trying to make it out.

"But, I'll never be able to answer the question— 'Have you ever been arrested?' —with a NO again."

"Would you like me to try and get your record expunged?"

"No, I don't think so." She let out a heavy sigh. "I think I'll eventually learn to live with it."

I love you. I love you. I love you.

That time, she got it.

Oh God, he was declaring himself by touch. No surprise, there. Touch was Aron's specialty. She didn't move. The sensation of him tracing those sweet words on her skin was infinitely wonderful. Should she react? Should she let him know she could tell what he was doing? He began speaking before she could decide.

"Can't you be satisfied with sexual adventures?" Aron sounded hopeful.

"My sexual adventures with you are always very satisfying." Honesty is the best policy. Usually.

He was still tracing that momentous phrase on her back.

120

I love you. I love you. I love you.

Every part of her body wanted to turn over and plaster herself against him, claiming the declaration and making one of her own. But, she couldn't. Not until she knew more about her remission. Maybe the tests that Doc Mulligan would perform in a couple of weeks would tell her if the remission was going to hold. If he said yes, she didn't know what she would do. "Libby?"

"Yes, sir?"

"Tell me what your dreams are?"

What could she say? Her walking-dream was asking her what her dreams were. "Let me sit up." Easily, he turned her and when she got her bearings, he had her cradled in his arms. "Honestly, I haven't spent much time dreaming."

"How can that be possible?" He traced that same little litany on the exposed skin of her chest, then rubbed her neck, sliding his hand on up to cup her chin. "A beautiful woman like you should have her dreams fulfilled as a matter of course."

"Thank you for saying I'm beautiful. Last night when I saw your ex-wife, I didn't feel beautiful at all. She's absolutely gorgeous." She buried her face in his hand.

"Sabrina can't hold a candle for you to run by. You are so far out of her league." Aron was emphatic. "She's passable...you are gorgeous."

"You're absolutely scrumdidlyumptious yourself." She held her face up for his kiss.

"Quit that." He laughed. "You're being cute because you're trying to evade the topic. Dreams, Libby–Lou, talk to me."

Start with something safe, she cautioned herself. "I've always wanted to make handmade designer handbags. I can sew and I have a knack for putting odds and ends together." She sat up straighter, getting a little excited in her description. "I like to take scrap material that I find in the sale bins at the fabric store, cut it out and sew it up and decorate it with buttons or beads or tassels—whatever. It's so much fun and each one is an original. A Libby-Lou Creation!" She smiled at him so sweetly, his heart rose in his throat.

"A Libby-Lou Creation?"

"Oh, I just made that up, because the words sound cute coming out of your mouth." He leaned over and kissed her.

"I like it. Okay, purses are dream number one. What else?"

"Well…" She ran one finger over the fine dusting of hair at the open vee of his black tight-fitting western shirt. Then, in a daring move, she began doing exactly as he had done before.

I love you. I love you. I love you.

He tensed at the feel of her finger, quickly looking down as if he could catch her at it. Their gazes fused and she picked her finger up and traced his lips. Aron trembled at her touch. "Tell me your dreams, Libby."

"I would love to go—" She stopped and turned in his lap, straddling him. He wrapped his arms around her and pulled her up until her breasts were pressed luxuriously against the hard muscles of his chest. Repeating, she began to whisper in his ear.

Aron was expecting to hear something totally outrageous. Instead, his throat muscles tensed as emotions battled for the upper hand. Adoration won—hands down. This is what she whispered, "I would love to go on a picnic—with you."

"A picnic? Libby, I'll take you on a picnic anytime you say. How about we do that and go out on the town to boot?"

As soon as he finished the sentence, she hopped a

little in his lap, which caused those stupendous breasts to bounce against him. Under her splayed femininity, his cock began to grow, seeking attention.

"Really? You would like to go out with me—in public?" He was stunned at her inference. Did she think he was ashamed of her? He didn't get a chance to defend himself; she started chattering like a magpie. "You'll have to take me to the bank so I can cash a check. I didn't bring any of my dresses with me." She didn't say that her dresses had all been old and too small. There was no use sounding totally pitiful.

"Sweetheart, when was the last time a man took you to dinner or out on a date?" He wanted to know, he just didn't want to know.

Libby thought for a second, and then answered. "Kevin Tucker took me out for pizza and to the video arcade when I was 15."

"That was ten years ago, Libby. What have you been doing for the last ten years?"

Heck! How was she supposed to answer that? Not truthfully, that's for sure. Unless…ah, the romantic approach. Truth, nonetheless. "Waiting for you."

"Libby…"

"If you don't have time to take me to the bank, maybe I can borrow the truck. I need to go grocery shopping, anyway."

"Why do you need to go to the bank?"

"To get money to buy something pretty to wear." Men were so dense.

"Why don't you have any money?"

His question was put out there and then he was silent. She didn't say anything, either. What could she say?

"Hellfire and damnation, Libby!" he yelled, almost dumping her from his lap. "Why haven't you said anything?" When she said nothing, he threw his hat clear across the room. "I haven't given you one red cent for what you've done at Tebow."

"I don't want anything." She announced quickly.

"What?"

"It wouldn't feel right."

"Why?

"Because..."

"Why?"

"Because it makes me happy to take care of you."

"Hell, Libby." Aron squeezed her tight. "I never expected you to come here and work yourself to death for nothing. You will accept the money, and I won't take no for an answer."

Libby grew still in his embrace.

"Okay?"

"I have an address you can send it to…"

"What address?"

"I have a debt I have to pay off."

Immediately, it crossed his mind that she might have debts like Sabrina ran up on him. "Credit card bills?" The tone in his voice sharpened.

"No, it's a student loan, sort of." She didn't mind him asking. Leaving his lap, she went and got her purse from the kitchen. Returning, she held up her bag. It was an attractive purse decorated with beads and leather. "See, I made this." Not waiting for a comment, she pulled out her wallet and handed him a slip of paper. "Just send whatever you were going to give me to this address."

Aron felt like a heel. He took the paper and jammed it into his front pocket without reading it. "Libby, I'm sorry about all of it."

"It's all right, Aron. I don't blame you. After what Sabrina did, you've got every right to be cautious."

"You've never given me any reason to doubt you in

any capacity." Aron was eating humble pie. "Do you feel like going to town now?"

"Don't I need to stay and fix lunch for everyone?" This was the first morning that she hadn't prepared breakfast for them in weeks. The boys hadn't known how to act when Aron had set out assorted cereals and milk. You'd have thought they hadn't eaten in a week.

"They can eat sandwiches."

"They won't be very happy."

"Who cares?"

***

Libby packed a knapsack Aron had given her with a few belongings. She was going camping! Today had been tremendously exciting. He had taken her to town and escorted her from place to place. They never made it to the bank, he said it wasn't necessary and they had started their round of shopping at a little boutique. Aron had gone crazy and much to Libby's chagrin he had bought her three complete outfits. She grumbled all the way down the street as he carried her packages.

"Get used to it. I intend to spoil you rotten."

The grocery store had been an adventure. Libby learned a valuable lesson; never take a hungry man to the supermarket. They ended up with four over-loaded, piled-high carts. One would have thought that on a ranch as big as Tebow they would butcher their own beef, but all of the cattle on the ranch were registered purebreds, and you don't eat show cows. So two of the carts were meat, almost exclusively. Libby loved to cook and Aron loved her cooking so he made sure she had every spice, herb and oil her little heart desired.

The longer the day wore on, the more Libby realized what she would be missing if she walked away from Aron McCoy. He made everything fun and every moment a joy. Being with him on an ordinary day was better than an adventure any day.

Chapter Seven

"You wanted to ride a horse, so come on Love, climb on." Aron held out his hand.

"Sultan is a really tall horse." Libby marveled. The golden Palomino stood sixteen hands high and weighed almost twelve hundred pounds. She placed her foot in the stirrup and he picked her up easily. "We're riding double?"

"Oh, yeah. We've got about an hour ride to the camp-site and I intend to have a helluva time with you." He sat her in front of him in the saddle. Aron was a big man, so the space between the saddle horn and his groin was snug.

"I like this." Her honesty warmed his heart. She had put her hair into a loose braid and he pushed it to one side so he could kiss her neck.

"So do I, so do I."

"We are going to be all alone, aren't we?" She didn't want anyone interfering in their time together.

"This is Tebow land, Libby. There'll be no one but us. I have a satellite phone in my saddlebag, if we need help. We won't see another living soul for the next two days."

"Maybe that's a good thing, considering the way I'm dressed." Libby didn't understand, but Aron had asked her not to wear pants—or underwear. He had spread a finely woven blanket over the front of the saddle, thereby making her a nice soft nest to sit on.

"You're dressed perfectly." She wore a red sundress that was now pulled up so high her bare bottom was nestled in the cradle of his thighs. The trail that Aron headed Sultan down was dappled in shade. "Look over there." Through a break in the copse of trees she could see a beautiful lake, and standing on the shores of the lake were hundreds of heads of longhorns.

"Wow, they're magnificent animals."

"Yes, they are. Big John, our oldest bull has an eighty inch spread to his horns, tip to tip. We raise them for breeding only and recently I sold a cow to a rancher in New Mexico for one hundred and seventy thousand dollars."

"Good Gracious!" She had no idea.

"I'm not a poor man, Libby." Aron didn't brag about his means, but he wanted Libby to understand he could take care of her.

"I know you're not, Aron." Raising both arms to touch his neck, she shifted in his arms for a kiss. "But I'm more interested in your non-financial assets."

"Good answer." How non-Sabrina could you get? "Time to get this show on the road." Without any warning, he pushed her elasticized sun dress down to her waist. Libby gasped in surprise and instant arousal. "Sultan knows the way." He doubled the reins and laid them across the horse's neck. "Lean back so I can have unhindered access to those beauties."

Gladly, Libby did as he asked. "I love the way your hands feel on my breasts. The little rough spots on your fingers make me want to wiggle. "

"Good to know my calluses are worth something to somebody." Aron let his hands slide up until he had picked both of Libby's tits up and lifted them until it would be possible to bring to life one of his sinful daydreams. "Lick them, Libby. Lick your pretty little
128

nipples."

"Me? That's your job?" Libby was perplexed. This, she had never even read about.

"They're right there, honey. You are bountifully blessed. Pleasure yourself for me."

With only a moment's hesitation, Libby bent her head and darted out her tongue to taste the tip end of her own breast. "Huh!" The sensation was not an unpleasant one.

"Now, the other one." She continued to follow his instructions. "Now, suck them for me." Aron's arousal went from atomic to nuclear at the sight of Libby's lips tugging on her own feminine flesh.

"Ummmmm," Libby mumbled as she sucked at the pebbled peak. It was the oddest sensation. Zing! This felt absolutely incredible. Tingles of pleasure were racing the two feet or so that separated her nipples from her clit. Without being told, she abandoned one nipple and latched on to the other one. Behind her, Aron chuckled.

Libby turned loose long enough to mumble. "Wow. If I'd known how good this felt, I would have been doing it all the time." At that revelation, Aron abruptly lowered her hands from her breasts.

"Oh, no. Forget, I introduced you to that wicked little pleasure. I refuse to be replaced," Aron laughed.

Still slightly dazed, Libby didn't realize what was happening until she felt herself being lifted and turned in the air. The next second, she found herself belly to belly with her man. "Now, it's my turn!" She began to unbutton his shirt. She was eager for more tactile delights. His hands fumbled with his belt buckle and zipper. When his actions registered with her, she looked up at him quizzically. "Is this even possible? Or safe?"

"I've never fallen off a horse in my life, Libby. And

129

I'm not about to start now. Trust me, Sultan and I will keep you safe." He pulled his cock from his pants and then proceeded to delve between her thighs with eager fingers. "Mmmmm, feels like you're already as slick and satiny as can be. Come here, love. Pull your legs up and put them around my waist."

With a minimum amount of contortion, Libby found herself maneuvered until she could gratefully slide down on his turgid cock.

Aron was already grunting with pleasure. "Now, this is an adventure, Libby-mine." She couldn't answer, all she could do was cling to his shoulders and coo with delight. In her position, and not wanting to spook the horse, the only movements she dared make were internal, but her efforts did not go unnoticed. "Damn, that feels unbelievable!" He buried his face in her neck and just wallowed in the wondrous rush of love that washed over him.

"Aron, open your eyes and watch where we're going. I can only see where we've been."

At her bossy little directive, Aron wiggled deep inside her. "You're not supposed to be able to process thoughts. Why aren't you mindless with rapture?" Who would have ever thought that sex could be so joyous? What used to be a necessary bodily function was now a celebratory event.

"I am mindless with rapture," she assured him as she rubbed her chest against his. "God, that feels good."

Aron was already leaking pre-cum and the tight fit of Libby's little pussy made him grunt with pleasure.

At her audible euphoria, Aron's level of arousal sky-rocketed. "Not going to last," he vocalized through clenched teeth. Standing up in the stirrups, and holding her upright, he rammed into her with tremendous force. Her ultra-sensitive pubis was grinding against his pelvic ridge, eliciting spurts of tremendous sensation. As she peaked, Libby reached out and bit Aron right at the point where his neck met his shoulder.

That was all it took, Aron roared with release. Bucking upward, he emptied himself within her, forever claiming her as conquered territory. Sultan pranced and sidestepped, but Aron did not falter or relinquish his hold on his beloved.

Libby felt no fear, only an absolute and utter elation.

Sinking back down, they cuddled and murmured little nonsensical phrases of praise and worship. The word love might not have been verbalized, but its presence was undeniable.

Teasing, Libby observed, "Sultan is so well behaved. This wasn't the first time you performed this equestrian feat, was it?"

"Actually, it was. Although, I will admit I have fantasized about it a time or two." Planting a smacking kiss on her forehead, Aron deftly reversed her position.

Sighing, she settled herself against him while he adjusted her clothes. "That was the most fun I've ever had on horseback, Libtastic." His manipulation of her name was becoming a precious oddity. She couldn't wait to see what else he would come up with.

"What is this, a Hilton resort?" Libby was shocked; she had expected a clearing and a campfire. Instead, there was a quaint, rustic cabin with mammoth rocking chairs on the front porch and a stone fireplace. There was even running water and a shower the size of a grotto. "Aron, this is tremendous!"

"It's the McCoy hunting cabin. Mom would go hunting with Dad and she didn't like to rough it. Dad wanted her company so he spruced it up for her."

"Your dad must have loved your mother very much." Libby didn't realize she sounded wistful.

Aron wanted to reassure her she was equally loved, but he also knew she wasn't ready to hear it. Something was holding her back. He suspected she had interpreted his skin-calligraphy the day before – and if he weren't certifiably insane, she had reciprocated. He fully intended to push the issue – sooner rather than later.

There was a complete kitchen and three bedrooms. The bathroom was downright luxurious, but the piece de' resistance was a king-size hammock which had been professionally engineered and securely hung between four strategically placed trees. Libby suspected the trees had been planted for this specific purpose. Walking up to the hammock, she began to have sensual visions. "Aron, after while...could we..."

"Make love in the hammock?"

"Oh, yeah." A nip on her butt caused Libby to levitate about eighteen inches. "Aron," she squealed. He had squatted down behind her, totally captivated by the way she was pulling on the thin cotton sundress she wore. Unconsciously, she had been fiddling with her dress, pulling it forward, leaving her bottom lovingly molded in thin see-through cotton. "Fooling around in this hammock is definitely on the agenda."

Aron had it all planned out. The fridge was stocked and he had changed the sheets on the bed. But, right now he had a couple of surprises up his sleeve. "Let's go, Precious."

"Where are we going?"

"Fishing."

"Do we have to use real live bait?" Libby pushed her bottom lip out in what was becoming his favorite expression – except for that dazed, rapturous look she got when she came apart in his arms, shivering in orgasmic ecstasy.

"What did you expect to use?" There was no chance he would lose his patience with her, she totally beguiled

132

him.

"A piece of wienie?" she looked hopeful.

"Lucky for you I brought some." He loped back to the cabin and came back with a wiener for her. The picturesque little lake was no more than a hundred yards behind the cabin and there was a dock built out over the watery expanse. He loved the way she looked with her legs dangling in the water.

He grinned, watching her push a piece of the meat-stick down over the hook. "You don't mind if I use a minnow do you?"

"No, but let me turn my head. I don't want to see you skewer it on the hook." She dutifully turned away while he baited his hook. Soon both of their lines were in the water, their bobbers floating on the surface.

Secure in his superior fishing capability, Aron announced. "The last one to catch a fish cooks supper."

"You're on, Buster." Libby accepted his challenge. They sat for a few minutes; enjoying the profound peace of the idyllic setting, taking joy in one another's company. Aron was leaning back on one arm, one leg propped up with one foot in the water. But, soon he felt a little hand nudging on his. "Can we hold hands?"

"Sure." He sat up, so she could reach him easier. She twined her fingers with his, then brought his hand over into her own lap and clutched it close. It was such a tender moment; Aron found himself swallowing back emotions he had never felt before.

"FUDGESICKLE!" Libby screamed, as she threw herself right on top of Aron. He had to scramble to catch her and still manage to keep both of their fishing poles from falling into the water.

"What happened, Baby?" He asked from underneath her.

"Something bit me!" she squealed.

"Where? Did a wasp sting you?" Aron held her and everything else was secure as his eyes searched her body for welts.

"No, it was a snake!"

"Libby, a snake did not bite you."

"Look!" she flounced to one side and held her lovely little leg right up in his face. He almost called a halt to their fishing to carry her up to the hammock and prematurely begin the sexual phase of their outing.

A light red mark did mar the creamy smoothness of her skin, but it was not a snake-bite. "Oh, Puddin', that's a perch-kiss."

"A what?" She pulled her leg into her lap to inspect the grievous injury.

"This lake is full of little white perch. They've always enjoyed nibbling on the legs and toes of unsuspecting humans who invade their domicile." Watching her study the little red mark was captivating, but when she bent down and kissed her own leg, he lost it. "Hey, you're treading on my territory, Precious."

Giggling, she looked up at him. "Well, you've got me kissing other parts of my body – I thought this wouldn't be out of line."

He leaned over and grazed his lips over the fast-fading mark. "There, now. Forget what I taught you earlier. I'll do all the Libby-kissing around here; I have no intention of being phased out as obsolete. Next thing I know you'll be using a dildo." He was just about to kiss his way to parts north, when Libby exploded.

"Look! Aron, look! I've got a bite!" Sure enough, Libby's bobber was going crazy. She grabbed her pole again and began a tug-of-war with whatever was playing with the hook.

"Wait. Wait. Let him get a hold of it real good, you want the hook to set before you pull your line out of the water." She followed his instructions, barely able to

134

contain her excitement. When the bobber completely disappeared, she jumped up and began backing up to allow her catch to emerge from the murky depths.

"Help me, Aron. I think I've caught a whale!" Aron laid his pole down, amused as all get-out. Standing up, he helped her pull in her catch. It wasn't a whale, but she had got a real good-sized bass. "Look at him!" Obviously, Libby was happy. And when Libby was happy, Aron was happy.

"Looks like I'm cooking supper." He pulled the fish up in a net, removed the hook and was about to slip the fish into a nearby cooler he had brought for this specific purpose.

"What are you doing?" There was a tinge of panic in Libby's voice.

"I'm putting him on ice, we'll eat him later."

"We can't eat Leon."

Aron sat back on his heels and looked at her. "Leon?"

"I don't think I could eat him. I've looked him in the eye, and he looked back at me."

Aron scrunched his lips together, desperately trying not to laugh. "Libby, this is not a catch and release lake. It's the McCoy fishing pond. And we eat our fish."

"Please? I'll do unspeakable things to your body." The devilish little gleam in her eye sold him on the concept.

"Come here, Leon." He readily grabbed the slippery fish and returned him to the lake. "Okay, baby – strip. Time for unspeakable things."

"Now?!?" Libby started to run, but Aron tackled her. "What are you thinking?"

"I'm thinking skinny-dipping. We're going swimming with Leon!"

"But what about perch-kisses?" Libby whispered

aghast.

"Perch ain't the only thing that's gonna be nibbling on you." Aron stepped back and began shedding his clothes hand over fist. Libby went more slowly, fascinated by the strip show he was putting on. When he was naked, she was captivated. His cock was so engorged and swollen it couldn't even stand up, instead, it hung heavy against his thigh. She felt her loins liquefy in anticipation of being filled by him.

He began to walk slowly toward her, she finished disrobing, stepping slowly backwards. She didn't know why she was retreating when everything she wanted was stalking her like a hungry predator. "You're going to step off the dock, Libbykins." he warned just a micro-second before she stepped off into nothing.

"RAT BUGGERS!" she squealed as her naked form was encased in the cool spring-fed water. Diving in behind her, Aron gathered her close, pushing her hair out of her eyes.

"Refreshing, huh?" She was so cute.

"It's colder than a witch's tit!" she exclaimed. The word 'tit' was the only word he heard, so he held her aloft in the water and fastened his mouth securely to one slightly wrinkled areola.

"Oh, I love that, Aron. Sometimes, I want to just sit in front of the television all night and let you lie in my lap and suck my breasts." The sexy domestic scene she painted had him designing blueprints in his mind. They needed their own house. He wanted to be able to love Libby anytime, anywhere without worrying about his brother's disturbing them. Or maybe, he would just build them another house – yeah that's what he'd do. He was the eldest – he'd keep the big house. Besides, Libby loved the house. It was fast becoming hers – not Bess's and not his own Mom's. Libby's.

"Mmmmm," he groaned as he chewed softly on her

nipple. "I could just eat you up."

He felt her legs wrap around his chest and she began to push against him in a rockin' motion that he longed to share. "Aron, I'm aching. I need you to put him in. Please," she begged.

"Relax and lay back," he instructed her. "You're going to float and I'm going diving." When he had her fixed, and she was lying on top of the water like some erotic mermaid, he brought his lips to her hot-button. With soft swirls, he caressed her pink folds. "You have the prettiest pussy."

"I'm going to sink, Aron. It feels too good, I can't be still." Aron ran his arms underneath her bottom and gave her the support she needed. He'd always give her the support she needed. Kissing her pussy was an absolute delight. She smelled like the body wash she used, something with raspberries. Tunneling deep in her passage, he felt her began to tense. Knowing she was close, he moved the sensual assault to her clitoris. Using the flat of his tongue, he laved the pink pearl until she screamed his name. Before she could recover, he stood her up and walked her to the dock. "Hang on, baby." Butting up to her back, he lifted her bottom and entered her from behind.

"My God, Aron." Almost immediately, she began to push back on him, enveloping him in red-hot velvet, enthusiastically impaling herself on his tumescent organ. "You are so big!" Enclosing one breast with a hand, he reached around her cupping her vulva in the other hand and finding her clitoris with the pad of his forefinger. Then, he went to work. Squeezing her breast, massaging her sex and pumping into her from the rear was a trifecta move. They had both been so heated with desire that in just a few minutes they were writhing in a climax so powerful, the tremors lingered and lingered long after the initial explosion. Without pulling out, he carefully turned her in his arms, running his hands over her damp body. She nestled close to him in complete trust and complete satisfaction.

Well, not completely complete. "I'm hungry, Aron."

"Well, since we won't be having fish for supper. How about a wienie?" Deep within her he wiggled his cock.

"Can we roast them, outside, around a fire?" The enthusiasm in her voice was contagious.

"Is there any other way?"

She was lovely by firelight. Aron couldn't take his eyes off of her. She had taken a quick post-romp shower alone, much to his dismay, and then changed into one of the short sets he had bought her. Seeing her clothed in things he had given her did something to the he-man part of him that wanted to provide for his woman. Her damp hair was loosely braided with a yellow ribbon and her eyes were shining like the brightest of stars. Tonight was the night. He was going to tell her he loved her or die trying.

She had been enthralled with roasting her own wieners on a limb that he had cut and carved just for her. In fact, she had almost made herself sick eating, because she kept wanting to hold another hot-dog over the crackling fire. "Hold off, Libby. Let's have dessert, instead." A warm look of lust came into her eyes and she reached for him.

"Wait, Munchkin. Hammock time is next, but while we've got the fire going, I want to introduce you to S'mores."

"That's what I want, too. S'more of you." He almost ditched the graham crackers and hauled her off to his lair, but he knew if he could calm her down she would love the warm chocolaty treat. And he wanted to give her every good experience he could think of. Libby's amazingly sweet innocence was riveting to him. Experiencing new things with her was like enjoying them anew for himself. Everything was fun. Every moment was precious.

"Here put these marshmallows on your stick." He handed her a couple of the big white fluffy ones.

With child-like awe she watched the puffy pillows turn brown, and then Aron showed her how to layer them on graham crackers with a small chocolate bar. The heat from the marshmallows would melt the chocolate and make the combination into a warm gooey sandwich of celestial goodness.

"Oh. My. God," she exclaimed when the flavors melted onto her tongue. "That's the best thing in the whole world!" Seeing his playfully downcast look, she relented. "Except you, of course." She ate two more before deeming it enough.

Catching him in an embrace, she cuddled him close. "Thank you Aron. I have never had this much fun in my whole life. I grew up in the city and never had a chance to do things like this. Later..." her voice trailed off, but she covered it up by letting her lips get preoccupied with kissing his. Aron's own mind was so preoccupied with his coming declaration, he didn't even notice.

"I'm glad you had fun. I enjoy every second I spend with you. There is nowhere else in the world I'd rather be, nor anyone I want to be with more."

"Take a walk with me. The moon is so pretty and full."

Who could resist a man like Aron McCoy? Sometimes when she looked at him, she couldn't believe he was hers. But, he was. By some miraculous means, this perfect man wanted her – Libby Fontaine. She took his outstretched hand, memorizing every feature of his beautifully chiseled face and body. Even though he was a physically perfect specimen, the most beautiful part of him was his heart. Plus, he was smart. And he loved his family; above all, he loved his family. Oh yes, she was lucky. "I'd love to walk with you, Aron."

He led her off the porch and out under the canopy of trees. A field of wild flowers lent its incredible scent to the fresh night air. A dove called in the distance and a lone owl added its haunting voice to the enchanted evening. They strolled past the lake and on down a narrow trail which led to a high bluff overlooking the grand expanse of Tebow land. "This is all McCoy property, Libby." He pulled her back against him and she laid her head on his wide chest. Aron rested his chin on her hair and his hands smoothed up and down her arms. "There is 535,000 acres of land in our holdings and we run nearly 20,000 mama cows for production purposes. We breed horses and cultivate our own hay and grain to feed them all. Primarily, our money comes from oil and natural gas."

Libby slowly stepped out of his arms. What was she doing here? This was a rich man. And who was she? Dirt poor, sickly Libby Fontaine. "I didn't know you had so much."

"Why did you move away?" He reached for her.

Libby held back, not moving to him as readily as in the past. "Aron, you could be with anybody! I have nothing, absolutely nothing to offer you. I am nobody, from nowhere. Why are you wasting your time with me?" Her voice was colored with despair.

Aron was flabbergasted. This was not at all what he had intended to convey with his speech. "Libby, you don't understand what I'm saying." He fell to his knees at her feet. "I have all of these things – this property, livestock, and minerals – but they mean nothing to me, nothing at all compared to how I feel about you."

Libby froze. God, it was happening. What was she going to do?

There were many things she could have done, but Libby decided she didn't want to look eternity in the face having lied to the man she loved. And, God, did she love this man. Taking one step forward, she knelt down with him – joining her hands to his. "I love you, Aron. So much." He held out his arms and she dove into them. Before he could respond, she slipped one hand over his mouth. "I've said it, now. I've told you how I felt, now let me finish."

He knew this was big, but he didn't know what was coming.

"You don't have to say you love me. I know you do. I can feel it stronger than I can feel my own heart beating, but I don't want you to say it out loud. Not yet." Aron moved his mouth under her fingers, needing to say something. "Let me finish." She took a deep, steadying breath. "There's something I have to do in a little over a week. Let me get through it, and if all is well, I'll come home to you. And when I do, the first thing I want to hear out of those sweet lips is how much you love me."

"And if all isn't well?" He had pulled her hand away, and was planting kisses in the soft well of her palm.

"I don't know, I just don't know."

"Why can't you tell me what's wrong? Don't you know I would turn the world upside down for you?" Aron's strong face was compelling; he looked as if he would slay dragons or attempt to pull the moon from the sky for her.

"There are some things beyond even your control, Aron." She grabbed both of his hands in hers and she kissed each finger. "But let me say it again, Sweetheart.

I love you. I love you so much. I never knew I would get the chance to say those words to anyone, so let me say them again. I LOVE YOU."

"Let me say it, Libby. For God's sake let me say it."

"No, don't. Things may fall apart. And if you say them, I would never be able to walk away from you."

"Is that why?" Aron was bamboozled. "If I were to say I love you, just saying that will prevent you from leaving me?" Could it be that simple?

"Yes, I'm afraid so."

Libby didn't understand that she was about to be hoisted by her own petard.

Aron rose swiftly, scooped her up and marched back toward the cabin. "Where are we going, Aron?"

"To the blasted hammock, that's where." He looked like a man on a mission.

Libby's heart raced with excitement. She was about to be thoroughly taken by the man she loved. When they reached the hammock, filled with gaily colored pillows and two thin blankets, Aron deposited her in the middle and then stood back. He began taking off his shirt. "Pull off those clothes, Baby. Skim them right off that sweet body. I know you don't have anything on under them, I've been watching the play of light on those puffy little nipples and that sweet shadow between your legs." Raising her hips and then her shoulders, Libby pulled the short-set off. Aron had undressed and he moved over her, blocking out the starlight.

"I'm about to show you how I feel about you, Libby-love." Aron whispered right in her face. "I'm about to worship you with my body." He nudged his nose up the side of her face, then back down. He ran his lips over her eyes and then he kissed the tip end of her nose. "A woman needs to know that she can't always dictate to a man about what he should do or what he should say."

"Really?" Where in the world was he going with this?

"That's right. I'm a man, Libby."

Duh! "Yes, you are." There was no denying that fact or the monster cock that lay up between them. Her private areas were already readying themselves for his possession; they sensed his presence and were preparing a place for him.

"I am your man."

She had no response to that, the knowledge was just too wonderful for words.

"And as your man, I have certain rights."

"Unalienable rights?"

"I don't know what those are." He thought for a moment. "Probably."

"I don't know what it means, either. Go ahead. Sorry, I interrupted you." She smiled. She loved him, so.

"Thank you." He paused. "Damn it, Libby. You made me forget where I was in my speech."

"You were saying, that as my man, (God, what a concept) you have certain rights. Unalienable rights."

He was resting almost on top of her, but he wasn't crushing her. To tell the truth, his proximity made her feel absolutely safe and protected. And the words he was saying were music to her ears. She had thought she didn't want to hear them, but she was wrong.

"Right. Unalienable rights. And one of those rights is to be able to share my heart with you, and my thoughts, and my feelings." He was so sweetly serious.

"Okay, I guess." Was he expecting her to disagree?

Good enough. Shifting her in the hammock, they lay side by side, facing one another. He skated his lips over her forehead, down her cheek and kissed her in the corner of her mouth. "I love you." His tone was so tender, it made her heart melt. This giant of a man was openly declaring his love for her like she was the most precious thing in the world to him. "Did you hear me, Elizabeth? I love you. I love you. I love you." As he said the words, he wrote them on the smooth skin of her back.

I love you. I love you. I love you.

"Yes, I hear you and I feel you." She leaned into him.

"So, what do you have to say?"

"I love you more than I love life." Loaded comment. "I'm honored above all women to be the recipient of your love." Then she grinned at him wickedly – "and my name's not Elizabeth."

"Not Elizabeth? Well, Libby-bell, what is your name? I think as the declared love of your life, I am entitled to that important piece of information."

"Can't you guess?" she teased. "You almost said it just a minute ago."

"What did I say?" He scrunched up his forehead, trying to recall.

"I know it's hard for you to remember, you talk all the time."

"Are you saying I rattle like a two-bit radio?"

"No, I didn't say that."

He pulled at her braid. "Now, what is the last name I called you. You're going to have to help me Libalicious, I'm getting old."

"Libalicious? I see a whole new phase of this game coming on."

He glared at her.

"Okay, you called me Libby-bell."

For a moment, he looked confused and then his eyes widened.

He still didn't say anything, so she sighed. "I feel

144

like my name should be Rumpelstilskin."

At his horrified expression, Libby convulsed in laughter. "I didn't say my name was Rumpelstilskin. Think, McCoy! Think!"

Holding her steady, so she wouldn't shake them out of the hammock, he finally said. "I got nothing."

"My name is Liberty. Liberty Bell Fontaine."

Aron roared. He laughed and laughed. He rolled out of the hammock and just had to walk away, laughing all the while. Libby almost got offended. "Hey, it's not that funny."

"Oh, yes it is. Suddenly it all makes sense."

"What makes sense?"

"How I've been acting."

"Run that by me again."

"You've had me chasing you around in circles. And I'm going to catch you and keep you, damn it, I'm entitled. It's my unalienable right."

"What right?" she was growing flustered.

He rejoined her in the hammock, cradling her close. "I am a man, Libby. And I am an American."

Oh, boy - here we go again. Was he about to sing, 'God Bless America'?

"And as an American man, I am entitled to life, Liberty, (that's you) and the pursuit of happiness."

A little while later the hammock rocked back and forth as Aron pumped hard within the loins of the woman he loved. She had her legs wrapped around him and her hips were working in tandem with his, meeting him thrust for thrust. The delicious friction of his cock sliding in and out of her body hit a spot deep inside of Libby that had her quaking with delight, an incredible sensation of heated desire coursing through her veins, his perfect movements sending flickers of raw carnal pleasure all the way to her womb.

Since Aron had told her he loved her, he had developed a voracious sexual appetite. His whole demeanor had changed, and he was more commanding, more demanding of her complete response and her utter surrender. It was as if he had conveyed to her that things had changed, she was now his possession, his responsibility. Libby moved her hands over his chest; she combed her fingers through his chest hair, feeling the small swelling of his nipples. She found this more than exciting. If it were possible she would have rose up into his body, crawled right up into him and made herself at home. Watching the play of emotions on his face, she longed to give back to him the same measure of pleasure he was giving to her. Impulsively, she sat up and mimicked one of his moves. Taking one of his nipples into her mouth, she began to suck on it, tonguing it, scraping it with her teeth. He let out a low, lusty growl, increased the speed of his thrusts and pushed his chest toward her, encouraging Libby in her sensual pursuits. "That's right, baby. Love me...love me with all you've got."

And so, she did.

Their mutual climaxes rushed upon them like a run-a-way mine train. Neither one of them had realized what a difference love made. But, it did. Love released energy and fed hungers. Love built bridges and tore down walls. Love settled doubts and answered questions. Love conquers all.

Chapter Eight

"Let's go in. That big old bed is going to feel really good." She held up her arms like a small child and he picked her up, heading to the cabin. They had dozed off, cuddled up. But the chill of the night air on his skin had awakened him. It was early morning, but they could still enjoy a few hours of sleep wrapped in the soft, warm covers. He had pulled on his jeans, but he hadn't bothered to dress her. They weren't going anywhere but straight to bed. Before he made it to the foot of the steps, he heard an engine.

Pulling up in the yard was Jacob.

As he got out of the pick-up, Aron turned to the side, shielding Libby from his brother's eyes.

He knew something was wrong. It had to be or Jacob wouldn't be here.

"You don't have the satellite phone on." Jacob quietly complained.

"Sorry. What's wrong?"

"Ya'll need to come home."

"What is it, Jacob?" Aron was getting scared.

"It's Joseph."

Libby threw their stuff together. The horse was to be left in the corral and one of them would come back for it later that day. She flew out of the bedroom and joined them as they hurried out the door and into Jacob's truck.

Aron had finally got out of Jacob that Joseph had been hurt. How badly, they didn't know. He had flipped his dirt bike in a freak accident during a race in Marble Falls. The family hadn't been notified immediately. Rather he had been airlifted to Dallas and was undergoing procedures to see what the actual damage really was.

"He takes too many damn risks." Aron suffered with the knowledge that his little brother's life might never be the same. "Is he paralyzed?" This was Aron's greatest fear. Since their parent's death, Joseph had become a dare-devil. Nothing was off-limits or too dangerous. Skydiving had been just one of the wild thrill-seeking interests which had drawn his attention. It wasn't that he had fallen in with a bad crowd. He existed on the periphery of these groups. He joined them for training and races, but did not immerse himself in their lifestyle.

Libby was sitting in between Jacob and Aron. She could feel the worry and tension emanating off their bodies. Any time one of the McCoy brothers was threatened or in trouble, they all rallied to defeat any adversary who might jeopardize their safety. Aron felt for Libby's hand, pulling her against him. "I'm so scared, Libby."

She turned, enclosing him in her arms, offering him all the comfort she could convey with her warmth and her embrace. "He'll be all right, he has to be."

When they pulled into the circular driveway in front of the main house, Jacob whipped his truck in and barreled out. Noah and Isaac stood on the front porch waiting for them. Nathan was nowhere to be seen. Aron helped Libby out and got her onto the porch. "Go in and check on Nathan. If you could put on a strong pot of coffee, I'd appreciate it. We've got to get things in line here and then some of us have got to get to Dallas."

148

"Anything, I'll do anything." She rose on tip-toe and molded her body to his. "Your family is more than important to me."

"Libby, you help just by being here." Giving her a hard kiss, he strode over to the others to see what the latest word was on Joseph.

Libby was devastated. All she could see in her mind was Joseph's beautiful face. He was so alive. Although like an addict, he constantly had to feed his need for the adrenaline rush he got from the high-risk adventures he lived for. All Libby could think about was how nice he had been to her and how much his brothers loved him.

As she started making preparations for their next meal, Libby began to feel ill. She stopped, afraid to move a muscle. 'No, God, no,' she prayed. From out of nowhere, waves of nausea caused her to break out in a cold sweat. She struggled to get to a chair. Holding her stomach, the panic hit her harder than the nausea. This felt so familiar. She knew what this was. Hello, old enemy. No, no, no. She wanted to run and just keep running—maybe she could outdistance herself from it. Hanging her head, she mourned what could have been. Libby had just found happiness and she didn't want to lose it so soon. Fleeing to the bathroom, she made it to the toilet just in time.

"Libby! Libby? Where are you?" Aron called. Hastily, Libby washed her face with cold water and dried it with a towel. Turning, she ran slap-dab into Aron's hard chest. He enfolded himself around her like a drowning man would cling to a life-line.

"Tell me everything," she encouraged, breathing in his scent as if it were the finest wine.

"He's awake, that's one good thing." His hold on her tightened, and he picked her up squeezing her to him. Libby would have groaned had she not known he was hurting worse than she was. "He's paralyzed, Libby. Oh, God, he's paralyzed." Tears dampened her neck. His tears.

"Oh, no." Libby cried. "How bad is it?"

"They are still running tests. I think he can move his hands and arms, but nothing below the waist." Aron rubbed his face back and forth over her shoulder as if trying to eradicate his painful reality.

"It could be a temporary thing," she sought to reassure him in any way she could.

"No one knows at this point." He let her slide down. "I'm going to go with Jacob and Isaac up to the hospital. Noah will stay here with you and Nathan to keep things going."

She took his face in her hands and rubbed away the trace of tears on his cheeks. "What can I do?"

"Pray, Libby," Aron begged. "I don't know how anymore."

"I will," she promised. "Anything else?"

"Take care of Nathan." Clutching her to him, he held her tight. "Oh, Baby... just knowing you're here and that I have you to come home to, makes all the difference in the world." Their lips met in a tender kiss. "I'll call you every few hours."

"Please, do. I want to know," she assured him.

"I won't be calling you just to inform you about Joseph, I'll be calling to get my Libby-fix. Sweetheart, I'm so sorry this happened just when we brought our love out into the light of day..."

"Don't worry, Aron. My love for you isn't going anywhere."

"And I don't want you to go anywhere, either. Whatever you have going on in your life that's creating this barrier between you and me—just know that I plan on beating the shit out of it. You will be mine, Liberty Bell. Do you hear me? And someday, I want to hear

150

exactly how you got that name." He tried to smile, but worry wouldn't let his face muscles relax enough to pull it off.

Libby's mind went back to the bout of nausea which had overtaken her only a little while ago. "Everything will work out. We just have to have a little faith."

"My faith is in you, Libby." He kissed her one more time before heading for the door, and Dallas.

***

Joseph lay in the hospital bed and wished he were dead. There was no way he could live like this. The doctors had tried to tell him the paralysis could be temporary due to swelling around the spinal cord. But they were only spouting off guesses. Hell, he couldn't even piss by himself. Every time a nurse came in and wanted to mess with the catheter that was stuck up his dick, he just wanted to throw a fuckin' bedpan at 'em.

Rolling his head from side to side, he tortured himself with a mental list of things he might never do again.

Ride a horse.

Climb a mountain.

Take a shit in anything besides a damn bag.

Walk.

Feel a warm, soft woman beneath him.

Get an erection.

Hell! Damn! Fuck! Joseph heard familiar footsteps coming down the hall - three sets of them. The steel-toed boots and the long determined strides of the McCoy brothers were unmistakable. In anguish, Joseph realized that he might never walk beside them again.

As the hospital room door creaked open, he reset

151

the muscles of his face into a devil-may-care expression. He couldn't let them know he was scared shitless. They didn't deserve to have to put up with a brother in his condition. He would have to see what he could do about that.

***

Libby had lain on the bathroom floor for about twenty minutes. She had kept the door locked. Now was no time to cause concern or generate questions—whether with Nathan or Noah. Concern over Joseph must come first. She had not let the time go to waste, however. She used it to reactivate her prayer life. She prayed for Joseph, that he would get well and go back to being the happy-go-lucky man they loved. Libby prayed for the family, that they would hold it together and be strong for Joseph. She especially prayed for Aron, asking God to encase him in a cocoon of warmth and peace. Lastly, she prayed for herself. Libby didn't want to die and leave Aron. Libby wanted to live.

When she was able to resume her work, she returned to the kitchen and put on a big pot of chili. The spicy stew would be perfect, because she could keep it hot and the guys could come in and eat it when they had time and felt hungry. Right now, it was her job to keep the house going and things as normal for Nathan as she could make them.

The phone rang a little after six. Noah grabbed it, anxious to hear news. He spoke quietly for a few minutes, and then handed the phone to Libby. She took the phone and Noah got up, giving her some privacy. "Hey, Baby." Aron's voice sounded tired.

"I love you, Aron." It was the most comforting thing she could think to say. "How's Joseph?"

"I love you, too, more than you'll ever know. I wish

you were here...I keep reaching for your hand. Jacob's slapped me twice. He thinks I'm getting fresh with him." Libby laughed at the mental picture. Aron's voice grew serious. "The tests are coming back, and the doctors say that Joseph has a spinal cord injury. They still can't tell us the full extent, but they know there is damage around the T10-L2 level."

"What does that mean?"

"I may be saying it all wrong, but right now Joseph seems to be fine above the waist, but he has very limited sensation below. That's not to say he won't regain some or all of it, but, right now, we just don't know. I can tell he is scared to death." Aron's tone revealed to Libby that he was worried and weary, also.

"What's next?" she asked.

"We're bringing him back to Austin in the morning. I want Dr. Cassidy to see him, as he's the absolute best. Oh, yeah, and I've called a contractor to come out and put in some ramps and do some work on the back wing to make a place for Joseph to have all the room he'll need...for...whatever."

Libby understood. Joseph's ordeal was going to be a long drawn out battle, at best.

"Tell him I love him," Libby whispered.

"I'll do it. You get some rest Libby-pearl. I'll kiss you awake when I get there."

"So, you're coming back tonight?"

"Yes, Jacob is going to stay and come back with Joseph when they transport him. Isaac and I are going to come home and then we'll all meet him at Brackenridge, tomorrow. They have a woman there that's supposedly doing wonders with patients like Joseph."

"Be safe," Libby said softly. "I'll leave the front porch light on."

"I will be, and Doll—keep the bed warm, I need you so badly. It just feels like if I could get my arms around you, everything would be all right."

"Hurry home, I'll be waiting."

Getting ready for bed, Libby made some decisions. Life was so uncertain, no one was guaranteed tomorrow. What happened to Joseph lent credence to that age-old truth. She decided that she was going to live as if God had sent her a memo and told her that she would break the century barrier. In a few days, she would keep her appointment with Doc Mulligan, but there would be no plans to leave Tebow until the day came when she felt that Aron was ready for her to go.

At the same time, she wanted to cover her bases and mend any fences that might have sagged over the years. Before she lay down, she wrote down the names of two friends she wanted to reconnect with, and she found a Bible in the den that she intended to read through—it had always been a goal of hers. Finally, she thought about making a will. That was funny; she didn't have anything to leave to anybody, except for her one precious piece of Aron's sculpture— 'Freedom'. And the only person she wanted to have that was its creator, Aron. If things looked like they were digressing, she wanted to put it back into his hands and see his face when she realized she had kept it safe for him all of these years.

***

Aron gently closed the door behind him. It was good to be home. The helicopter carrying Joseph and Jacob had probably beaten them back to the Hill Country. As soon as morning came, they would head to the hospital as a family. A Dr. Susan Grigsby was going to sit in on the consult with Cassidy and they would

154

evaluate Joseph's test results and recommend what would come next. One thing which worried Aron was the thought of Joseph having to exist in a sterile hospital setting. That was why he intended to build whatever facilities were needed for Joseph to rehabilitate at home. While the contractors were at it, he was going to build a studio for Libby—a place where she could design and create her handbags. It was good to have contacts. He had placed a few phone calls to a man he knew in New York, and soon boxes and boxes of fabrics, decorations, leathers, and all manners of sewing supplies would be delivered to the front steps of Tebow. He had also told Gregory to send state of the art sewing machines and sergers so Libby would have the very best tools to work with. There was nothing too good for his love, and he couldn't wait to see her eyes light up when she saw his surprise. It would all come to pass quickly, because Aron wanted things to settle down and get back to some semblance of normal. Joseph was going to be all right...Aron was determined he would be. Nothing else was acceptable.

Heading up to bed, he found her right where she belonged. "Now, that's what I needed to see." He breathed a sigh as he took in the sight of Libby in bed, curled up on her side. Her hand was underneath her cheek, and the covers were thrown back to reveal the fact that she was waiting on him wrapped only in the beautiful skin God had originally clothed her in. Stripping, he was eager to feel her warmth merge with his.

"Libby-honey, open those arms, I'm home." Immediately, she opened herself to him, fitting her body to his, welcoming him home.

"I'm so glad you're here. How's Joseph?" She didn't give him time to answer. She was so starved for the taste of his kiss that she molded her lips to his and drank greedily. Aron answered in kind. Rolling to his back, he pulled her on top of him, letting his hands move down her body, memorizing every dip and hill. He plunged his tongue in deep, letting it mate with hers. How wonderful it was to be greeted with a homecoming like this.

So glad to be with her, Aron felt playful. Running his hand down her silky back, he let his fingers play lower. Her sweet bottom was beckoning him to caress and mold. Dipping his finger between the clefts of her cheeks, he teased regions that had as of yet gone unexplored. She gasped at the unfamiliar intrusion. Aron just laughed, "Nice crack, Liberty Bell."

Not to be out done, she came back with one of her own. "Why don't you just give me your John Hancock, already?"

"So, you want me to dip my feather in your ink?" Their happy laughter filled the room.

"I'm sure there's a law against patriotic porn on the books somewhere," she teased.

"Just as long as there is no law against loving you." Aron put his hands under her arms and lifted her up, sliding her body over his until he could get one of her nipples in his mouth. Without preliminaries, he began to suckle, seemingly taking comfort from the feel of her breast in his mouth. Libby lay her head on the pillow above his, relaxed, enjoying the tug and pull of his lips and the rasping of his tongue. In a moment, his fingers found her sex and he began to massage her slit, sliding his finger in and out, reminding her why she had been created. His mouth became insistent on her breast, demanding an audible response to his lovemaking. She gave it to him.

"You are making me crazy, Aron." She tightened her sheath around his fingers, moving her hips in a dance of excitement. Pulling one nipple out of his mouth, she shifted and offered him the other. He never missed a beat, consuming the jealous nipple with a devotion equal to what had been lavished on its counterpart. "Bite me, please – just a little."

Chuckling under his breath, and without turning loose of her breast, he nipped at her nipple. The sharp jolt of erotic shock ripped through her, making her wonder at the depths of sexual exploration still available for them to delve into. "Oh, I like that," she praised him. "You are so good."

"Can't wait any longer," he announced. Guiding her to one side, he rolled them over, careful to keep his full weight from crushing her. "Open those legs, Libby. I need to come inside."

Splaying herself open, she lay there eagerly awaiting him. "I ache Aron, fill me up, please." Libby lifted her hips to him, panting for his possession. Slowly, he pushed in. He seemed larger than usual, bigger around, more swollen. She felt her channel stretching to make room for his tremendous girth. Every nerve ending in her vagina was tingling with high-pitch awareness. Even the lips of her vulva were passion-kissed with arousal, seeking to fit themselves around his member, making them one in body as well as spirit.

"Look at me, Libby," Aron demanded as he sank further into her. She lifted her amethyst eyes to him, but they were unseeing, unaware of anything but the wonder of his claiming. "Do you know who you belong to, Libby?"

She managed to nod, but she couldn't verbalize a response. Aron thrust into her hard, as if he were planting a flag, claiming his property. "You are mine, Liberty Bell. I don't want there to be a doubt in your mind." Sitting back on his haunches, he pulled her up and across him, lifting her hips, angling her so that he would drag sensuously across the very place which would drive her insane.

Taking complete control, Aron thrust into her again, slowly, rubbing the distended purple glans at the head of his penis across the spongy spot that was made for just a time as this. What a marvel the human body was, she managed to think. She was created just for him, fashioned to accommodate his male needs and demands. "Mine, Libby. Mine," he chanted as he drove into her, pushing as deep within her heart as he was into her body. He laid his hand flat on her belly, steadying her for his pummeling. Unable to contain the bliss, Libby shattered into a million shards of light and color. Her body fluttered and pulsed around his staff, massaging his phallus until he too, flamed and detonated, pouring himself into her with unequaled vigor. Even after he had emptied himself, Aron kept rocking into her, unwilling to pull out and break the sweet connection.

"I love you, Aron." Libby said it like a prayer, a fitting benediction to a sacred act.

"I worship you, Baby. You don't know what it meant to me, knowing you were here waiting for me." He moved from over her, fitting himself to her back, pressing against her, asserting himself as her protector.

"Can I go with you to see Joseph tomorrow?" she asked, holding her breath. As far as she was concerned, this was a test. Did he consider her a girlfriend or a bedmate?

"Of course. He's already been asking for you. He wants some of your brownies." Before he knew what was happening, she was out of the bed. "Hey!"

Smacking him on the forehead with a loud kiss, she calmed him. "Go to sleep. I'll be back in an hour and a half. If Joseph wants brownies, then he gets brownies." Aron knew there was no use arguing with her. Libby had made up her mind.

As she padded down the stairs, Aron lay there and counted his blessings. Libby made life worth living. If only Joseph were whole again, life would be perfect. Throwing the covers off, he went to the sink and wet a washcloth and wiped off the remnants of his passion. Only six weeks ago, he had been alone and lost, bitter in his celibacy. He had only dreamt of having a companion like Libby—one who was sweet, sexy and eager to show him her love. Stroking himself, he remembered the wonder of Libby's heat engulfing him and he prayed to God that Joseph wouldn't have to go through life and never experience this kind of joy.

When the brownies were done, Libby returned to Aron's arms. Without awakening, he instinctively made a place for her, whispering her name and nuzzling her neck. Before sleeping, she sent up another petition that she be given the gift of health and life so she could spend her days caring for and spoiling the man that she loved.

***

Libby and Aron entered the hospital room expecting to find an invalid; instead they found an agitated, unhappy McCoy—which is a fearsome thing. "I want to go home, Aron." Joseph demanded.

Even as he bellowed at his brother, he held his arms open to Libby. She sat the brownies down on the rolling table and hurried to step into Joseph's hug. "How are you?" she whispered for his ears only.

"Holding up," he whispered back.

"I'm getting you out of here as fast as I can," Aron assured him. "I've got two crews who will be there today and they are making all the modifications necessary so we can get you set up for anything you may need."

"Sounds good to me. I'll go crazy if I have to stay in this place very much longer."

"Can I get you anything?" Aron asked.

"How about some coffee to go with those scrumptious smelling brownies?" Joseph wanted to get Aron out of the room. He needed to talk to Libby.

Aron left for the coffee, willing to do anything that would perhaps bring a smile to his brother's face. Once the door shut behind him, Joseph sobered. "Libby, you've got to do something for me."

Libby didn't like the change in his demeanor or his voice. "What would that be, Joseph? You know I'd do anything to help."

"I want the truth. I need you to find out from Aron exactly what my expectations are. They're just feeding me a line of bull. I know I'll never walk again…there's no way. I can't feel my feet. Hell I can't even feel my balls unless I reach down to see if they're still there. I don't know if I can face life as half a man, Libby." He sounded so desperate; she knew he wanted to scream in frustration. Libby knew exactly how he felt. She had felt the exact same way that very day.

Even though it shouldn't be so, with a man it was different. Libby recognized the symptoms. She had seen it more than once. A man's identity was so tied up in his strength, how tall he stands, and in his virility. She heard panic in his voice, raw panic that could eat away at your sanity and leave you questioning the value of facing another day. Joseph was questioning his legitimacy as a human being. This scared the crap out of her. She had to get through to him.

"Joseph Anthony McCoy, you listen to me—and you listen to me good." Libby got right up in his face, desperate to make him understand. "Life is worth living, in whatever state you're offered it. I'm going to level with you. Aron doesn't know this yet, and I shouldn't be telling you before I tell him…but this is an emergency, so…here goes. I have spent the last eight years of my life living on borrowed time." At Joseph's puzzled expression, she sat down beside him and took his hands in hers. "At present, I am in remission. My disease of choice is leukemia. The type I have is fairly aggressive and remission doesn't usually last over two years. Yet during this unexpected and perhaps brief reprieve, I have fallen head over heels in love with your brother. He wants a future with me, a future I have no assurance even exists."

Joseph was flabbergasted. "Libby, you have cancer?" Pulling her to him, he held her close. "No, you've got to be all right! We can't do without you."

"Exactly, my point—and we can't do without you!" she spoke in an adamant, no-nonsense tone. "Joseph, I have hope. It may be stupid, but I don't have a choice. In one week, I'll go and sit down in front of a doctor and he will tell me whether my blood count is still improving or whether it is taking a nose-dive. Just yesterday, I had waves of nausea knock me to my knees. Yet, I can't give up. I want to live too badly to throw my hands up and quit. I love your brother, and I want to live for him. And you, you don't know what the final verdict is, yet. You have to get a grip and find a way to hold on. Joseph, you have got to have hope, also. Your family loves you. I love you. And, there's a woman out there— somewhere, that was meant just for you. She's not here yet, but she's coming. Love is worth holding on for."

Libby could tell she had hit a sore spot. He looked at her sadly. "I don't have anything to offer a woman, Libby. My injury has stolen my manhood."

"Don't say that, Joseph." She clasped his hands. "Let's make a pact. I'll pray for your miracle, if you pray for mine."

"Deal?" She waited, expectantly.

He hesitated for a few long moments. Finally, he answered, "Deal." Solemnly, they shook on it. This is the way that Aron found them.

"I just leave the room, and come back and you two are all lovey-dovey. Should I be jealous?" he asked with a smile.

"Yes, you should." Joseph kissed Libby on the forehead soundly. "If the day ever comes, when you don't want her—I'll be standing, hopefully, standing by."

"I want you standing, Joseph…walking, running, jumping…whatever." Aron assured him. "But you can't have my Liberty Bell."

"Your what?" Joseph wasn't privy to Libby's real name.

"Liberty Bell Fontaine," Libby explained with a smile. "My mom was from Philadelphia, and about the time I was born, I think she was feeling homesick."

***

Libby cooked and cleaned around the mess the contractors were making. The hustle and bustle of revamping the back wing of the Tebow main house was exciting in a way. It meant that Joseph could come home as soon as possible, and they could care for him. Libby was nervous. She had endured two more bouts of nausea, complete with throwing up.

But instead of giving up, she was determined to have a positive attitude. Oddly enough, her puniness only seemed to affect her after breakfast, and by noon it was over and she would feel fine. Aron wouldn't let her go back and inspect the work being done. He told her she might get hurt, and on top of that, he wanted it to be

162

a surprise. Why he wanted to surprise her, she didn't know. The work was being done for Joseph.

No one had thought to do it, so Libby did—she called Bess and broke the news to her about their sweet dare-devil. Libby had thought long and hard about calling her. She halfway expected for Bess to say she was on her way back to Tebow and Libby wasn't certain she wanted that. She wasn't ready to leave. Aron might want her to stay, but there were still doubts floating around in her head.

Bess was shocked, to say the least. She said she would call Joseph, but she didn't offer to come home. In fact, she talked as if Libby's time there was indefinite. That sounded like music to Libby's ears, but there was still the dreaded doctor's appointment to get through.

***

The work was complete, and Libby couldn't wait to see what Aron had done to accommodate his brother. She had so much planned...they all did, and everyone was anxious to have Joseph home. She had gone to see him almost every day and each time they were alone, Joseph questioned her about how she was feeling. The doctor's appointment was the day after next, and Joseph's support was one of the main things keeping her going. She still hadn't confided in Aron. She just couldn't bring herself to do it. After seeing Doc Mulligan, she would know what she was going to say, anyway.

There were plans to bring Joseph home that very afternoon, so Libby began cooking all of his favorites. She decided to make it her personal mission to keep his spirits as high as possible. At the stove, she worked on a pot of homemade chicken noodle soup. Adding some parsley and cream, she put it on a slow simmer. When two large, warm hands slid around her waist, she didn't even start, his touch bringing her the greatest comfort in the world. Leaning back against him, she breathed a sigh of contentment. "I'm so glad Joseph is coming home." As soon as she said the words, she almost bit her tongue. She had to be careful…she was beginning to talk as if this were her permanent home and she was the matriarch or something.

"Yeah, me too." Kissing the back of her neck, he teased, "You smell almost as good as your soup." Pulling her gently by the hand he walked her to the rear of the house. "Close your eyes. I've got something to show you."

"They're closed. It smells good in here. I love the 'new' stuff smell." Aron was right behind her, his hands moving up and down her arms. When they stopped, he moved to her right side. "Okay, open them." Libby did. For a moment, she didn't understand what she was seeing. This wasn't what she was expecting—not at all. Where she was prepared to see exercise equipment, massage tables, whirlpool baths, and stuff like that— instead, she saw shelves and work tables. Libby put her hand over her mouth and walked forward. There was a sewing machine and a serger. There was equipment to attach jewels and studs. And the wildest part was that the shelves were full of every type of material and fabric imaginable. Boxes of beads, jewels, brads, studs…all types of decorations were in neat little cases. There were scissors and tape measures, threads and cording, enough to make any designer cry. Sweetest of all was the sign on the wall. "Libby's Designer Bags."

Libby began to cry. Turning, she blindly groped for him. She didn't have to move but a few inches when he pulled her close. "Do you like it, Baby?"

"You did this, for me?"

"I'd do anything for you, Libby-mine." This was fast becoming his favorite Libbyism. Libby's tears were not fading; in fact she was beginning to sob. Aron didn't know what to do. This was supposed to make her happy—not sad. "Hey, hey." He scooped her up. "Why in God's name are you crying, Sweetheart?"

Little hiccups of tears interfered with her speech patterns.

"What….about….if….I….have….to….leave?"

"Leave? Libby, you're not going anywhere."

"I may not have anything to offer you." She sobbed into his shoulder.

"What do you mean? You have the only thing in the world that I want."

"What is that?" More hiccups. More tears.

"You."

You. His love for her was a miracle. Dare she hope for two? "I may not be able to stay forever."

"I don't know what that means, but I won't settle for anything less. Forever is the only thing that will do. Forever is all I want. It's the only thing I will accept."

She framed his face with her hands and began to smother him with kisses. The passion that always smoldered between them flared up. "Let's christen my sewing table," she suggested with a twinkle.

He carried her over to the wide wooden surface. "Good suggestion, Babe. It's just the right height."

"Right height for what?"

"For this." He laid her down, pushed her skirt up and ripped her lace panties off with one sharp tug. "Do you know what I want to do?"

"Yeah, probably." She hoped.

"I want to shave you. Will you let me?"

"What?" This was a surprise.

"I want you smooth as silk. Do you trust me?"

"With my life." That wasn't a lie.

"Lay right there." He was gone 94 seconds, she counted. When he returned, he had a towel, a razor, some shaving cream and a wash cloth.

"Heavens to Betsy!" she gasped.

"That's right, Libby, I'm about to shave you till you're smooth and soft as a baby's bottom." He proceeded to do just that. With great care, he dampened the area, applied shaving cream and began to pass the sharp blade over the delicate, down-covered skin. She tensed up, not really expecting it to hurt, but fully aware this was a totally new experience. Trust Aron to make it a spectacular experience! He would shave a spot, wipe, then kiss—shave a spot, wipe, then kiss. By the time he had her naked, she was wet and ready for some extra special attention. Aron went a little crazy; he rubbed his face across her smooth mons, bumped her clitoris with his nose and tongued her thoroughly from one end of her slit to the other. By the time he had made two passes, Libby couldn't remember her own name.

"Aron, I swear to God, if you don't get inside of me right now, I'm going to scream." Libby panted with desire. When Aron hesitated, stripping off his clothes, Libby scooted her bottom down the table and made a grab for his business.

Aron dodged, just for fun. "Do you want something Libby-mine?"

"Yes, I do." She made another pass at him, again he side-stepped. With a wicked gleam in her eye, Libby decided to change tactics. She knew this would work; it had certainly paid off at the stock tank.

Opening her legs, she showed him what he was missing. Thanks to Aron, she was as smooth as silk. Pink, glistening and swollen, it felt as if she were actually pulsing down there. Never taking her eyes off of him, she sucked on her forefinger really slow. Aron almost stopped breathing. She had his attention. Taking the wet, glistening finger, she rimmed her pussy lips, enjoying the new-found smoothness. A little hum of satisfaction escaped her mouth. Aron moved one step closer. Making one circle around her clitoris, Libby made hungry little grunting noises, specifically designed to make Aron sorry he had started the teasing game. "You can go back to work Aron, I've got this one," she spoke in a husky tone. Ignoring the movement she heard at the edge of the table, Libby moved her finger down her slit to the opening that was swollen and puckered, like a hungry little mouth. Sliding her still wet finger inside of herself, she wiggled it around and moved it in and out, letting her hips gyrate to a tune that only she could hear.

"Good God, Libby," Aron breathed.

At his tortured tone, she added another dimension to the performance. Moving her hands away from her pussy for a brief respite, she plumped her breasts and began to tease them. "They want to be sucked, Aron." Taking her nipples in her fingers, she pulled on them, distending them out, then rolling them around between her thumb and forefinger until she drove her own self mad. One hand ventured back down to her desperate little hole, and she slid in – adding another finger to the first, pushing rhythmically in and out of herself until she moaned in pleasure.

"Stop. Stop." Aron ordered. "You're killing me." He clasped both of her hands and stilled their movement. Grabbing her ankles, he pulled her right to the edge of the table and plunged in. There was no preliminaries, no introductions, no warning. Libby literally screamed with relief when he began to hammer inside of her. "You shouldn't tease," he admonished as he gave her just what she craved.

"Good God, Libby," Aron breathed.

"I don't know why not," she panted, "I seemed to be getting what I deserve." Her rapier wit, even in the midst of a good romp amused him no end.

"Oh, you think so, do you?" He didn't know how long he could keep up the banter, but he didn't want to be the first one who slipped into mindlessness. "I think you deserve better than this."

"What do you think I deserve?" He picked up one leg at a time and placed them up on his shoulders. Kissing her ankle, he ran his hands up and down her legs.

"I think you deserve to be deeply and completely – " he paused for effect. Libby thought he was about to talk dirty to her, but instead, he almost made her cry. For the word he growled, was the most precious one he could have enunciated – "loved."

At his sweet words, she lost it. No longer able to say anything, she just laid back and enjoyed herself. The feeling of him loving her was the most wonderful sensation she could ever hope to experience. No doubt about it, she felt taken, possessed, conquered. But mostly, she felt cherished. Her climax overtook her and she trembled like a leaf in a hurricane. "Aron, Aron," she moaned. "Don't stop, for God's sake, don't stop."

He couldn't have stopped if the world had been grinding to a screeching, apocalyptic halt. The feel of her fisting around him in convulsive, tiny movements made him swell until he thought he would literally burst. She watched him take his pleasure, she watched him throw his head back and bow his neck. God, she loved him. She adored him. Wanting to see the wild side of the man she craved, she whispered, "Show me your teeth, Baby." When she said that, he did—he bared his teeth at her and drove inside of her like a raving madman with a jackhammer. Nipping her ankle, he raised her

168

bottom clear off the table and spewed his life-giving essence deep inside of her, marking her forever as his choice.

Needless to say, Libby appreciated her design studio.

Later, he shared with her the haven he had created for Joseph. Now, when they had him home, they would be on the road to recovery.

Chapter Nine

"I hate to bother you Aron, but did you send any money to that address I gave you?" Libby didn't want to have to ask, but if he'd changed his mind, she was going to have to get to the bank and move some money. The last thing she wanted to do was miss a payment to the foundation which had been so generous to her. If it hadn't been for them, she wouldn't have been able to finish school or take the college classes she had enjoyed so much. One day, if her remission held, she was going to finish her degree.

They had spent the day readying Joseph's room for his return. The guys had put handrails in the bathrooms and installed a chairlift on the stairs. Isaac had even moved the furniture around in the den and dining room so Joseph's wheelchair would be able to maneuver through the area easier. Aron had just finished a ramp that would ease Joseph's getting on and off the verandah. Finally, everything that needed to be done for their brother's homecoming had been completed. Libby had walked out to bring him a big glass of iced tea, which he drank thirstily.

Aron looked sheepish. "I'll take care of it as soon as I put up my tools. I've had so much on my mind. I'm sorry I forgot." He picked up her hand and kissed her.

She had tried to hide it, but Libby was pale, and her skin was slightly damp. Aron was a little worried about her. Maybe, she was just nervous. She still hadn't told him what the big trip to Austin was about at the end of the week. He knew it was momentous for her, and all he could think of was that she had some type of court appearance or legal problem. She had said there was a battle and an enemy and Aron couldn't think of any other possibility. All Libby would have to do was ask, and Aron would have a battalion of lawyers at her disposal. He was fairly confident it was no big deal, or Libby would have been upfront and honest with him about it. Still, he knew it was important to her, or she wouldn't have gauged their relationship by its boundaries. Whatever it was, she wanted it out of the way before she gave their future a green light.

Libby returned inside and Aron cleaned up his work area. When he entered the house, he looked for Libby and found her curled up on one of the couches in the den. She had dozed off. Lifting her, he carried her to their room and laid her on the bed. At the contact with the mattress, she roused. "Aron, when you come to bed, will you get my fuzzy slippers from the bottom of Bess's closet?"

"Sure thing, Babe. Let me take care of that bill for you and I'll be right back." He intended to do an electronic transfer if he could find the information online. Heading to his office, he found the slip of paper which was still folded, just as she had handed it to him. Sitting down at his computer, Aron flipped the power switch and sat back till the monitor woke up. Taking the paper Libby had given him, he unfolded it and looked at the address. His heart immediately rose up into his throat. The recipient was The Rockwell Foundation. His parent's legacy. This was his company. With shaking fingers, Aron logged into the Foundation Website and

172

entered the account number on the paper.

One Liberty Bell Fontaine had been granted a loan of five thousand for tuition, books and fees. She had made ten payments which had all been mailed on time and in full. Aron's heart was beating a mile a minute. There had to be some mistake. This grant money was only available to those adults who were attempting to get their education while battling cancer. Throwing the paper down as if it burned his fingers, he paced up and down the floor.

There was nothing to do, but go ask her. Surely, there was some explanation. Perhaps she'd gotten the loan in her name, but it was for someone else, someone else who had cancer. It had to be. Throwing open the door to his office he started to his bedroom to beg her to explain the mistake. Halfway there, he remembered the slippers. With shaking hands, he opened Bess's door and went to the closet. There on the floor were the pink bunny slippers which would keep her feet warm. Kneeling down, he reached for them. His hand bumped a pasteboard box which contained something quite heavy. Wondering at its contents, he pulled it to him. Opening the box, he stared at the contents dumbly for a moment, until what he was seeing registered with him.

It couldn't be.

It just couldn't be.

Aron doubled over in pain.

No! No! No! He screamed in his head.

Aron's first bronze was in the box, cradled by a generous nest of tissue paper. Everything the PI had said flashed back through his brain. The buyer of 'Freedom' was someone Martinez had seen on television. The buyer of 'Freedom' was a woman who was battling cancer. Leaving the bunny slippers where they lay, Aron stumbled to his feet. He had to get out of the house.

Now.

Not seeing anything, he plowed through the house, staggering through the door and out on the porch. Still not aware of his destination, Aron began to run. If he ran fast enough, he could get away from the truth. If he ran far enough, he could escape the horror that Libby was sick, maybe dying.

God, Libby had cancer.

Damn! Damn! Damn!

She had told him time and time again . . .

You don't have to say you love me.

I'll stay until it's time for me to go.

I may not be able to stay forever.

I don't have anything to offer you.

Holy Jesus! He was going to die, right here.

Aron fell to his knees and screamed at the top of his lungs.

"No! No! No!"

First his parents – and Lord in heaven knew he'd prayed they would be found alive. But, no. Three days after their car had been washed off the bridge, their bodies had been found, still trapped in their watery grave. Joseph was paralyzed and Aron's prayers had not changed any of the test results. And now his precious Libby was sick.

What was he going to do?

What had he done?

Aron beat the ground with his fists. He had given his all for his family. Never had he even considered backing away from them or throwing his hands up. He had always put others first.

"Libby! Oh, God – Libby!"

Aron cried until he couldn't cry anymore.

Libby was so cold and sick. Shaking, she made her way to the bathroom. "Aron!" She called. "Aron, where are you?" There was no answer. The house was quiet.

174

Jacob, Isaac, Noah and even Nathan were out with the wranglers finishing up the vaccinations and the branding of the weaned calves. They probably wouldn't be in until the wee hours of the morning. There had been no one in the house but them. Now Aron was gone. She made it to the bathroom, but she couldn't sit up. So, she lay down on the floor near the tub. She would rest her eyes, just for a moment. Then, she would feel better.

Aron sat out under a spreading pecan for over an hour. He had to get control of his mind and his body. Reasoning with himself, he went over his options. Clearly, he had to get Libby to talk to him. Obviously, this had everything to do with the secret appointment she had to keep. Why hadn't she told him? Aron felt betrayed. Didn't she trust him?

What did this mean for them? Holding his head in his hands, Aron tried to think. Offering up one prayer after another, he asked God to calm him enough so he could make the right decisions. Rocking back and forth in agony, he waited for a sign.

Little by little, peace flowed into his soul. And with the peace came a modicum of clarity. It was easy. Libby was his gift from God, so therefore God must intend for him to have her and keep her. They could face this together. They could beat this together. With that revelation easing his mind, Aron went back to the house.

Libby was scared. She felt so bad. Where was Aron? Finally, she heard footsteps coming down the hall. When they entered the bedroom, she heard them pause. He was looking for her in the bed, only she wasn't there. "Libby? Baby?" Walking the few short steps to the bathroom he spotted her. "Baby, oh God!" Kneeling beside her, he lifted her in his arms.

"Would you take me to the doctor, Aron? I'm sick. I feel so bad." Her voice was so small, yet the request was so momentous. Taking just a millisecond to cleave unto her, he vowed to God to do whatever it took to keep her.

He radioed for Jacob. There was no way he could drive and hold her at the same time. And he needed to hold her.

"I'm sorry, Aron." Libby whispered.

"Shhh, Baby." He comforted her. "Everything is going to be okay."

Before long, they were headed to the hospital. Mulligan had been called and he would meet them there. Mulligan! Damn, he should have recognized his name. He was the Chief Oncologist at Brackenridge. Hell, Aron was on the board, but apparently he wasn't on the ball. The name hadn't even rung a bell with him.

"I should have told you," Libby continued to try and make amends. "I thought I would get to feeling better." She held on to his shirt with a tight little fist and buried her head in his shoulder. "I've been living with leukemia for years." When every muscle in his body tensed, she began rubbing his chest and arms and shoulders, anything she could reach. "I've been in remission and I didn't want you to know anything about it until after my check-up." Aron rubbed his lips back and forth across her forehead. When he didn't say anything, she sought to find more words to say to make it all better. "If you don't want to come with me, I'd understand. Who wants to wait at the hospital while all those tests are being taken?"

"Where else would I go, Sweetheart?" Aron asked. His voice was stiff with unshed tears. "My place is by your side. And that's where I'm going to be."

Jacob drove carefully, but at a pace designed to eat up the miles. He kept glancing in the rearview mirror, willing Libby to feel better.

"You knew about this, didn't you? You son-of-a-bitch," he bit out at Jacob, once he realized Libby had dozed off. It had just registered with Aron that this was the secret Jacob had kept for so long.

"Yeah, I didn't want to. But, she begged me to keep her secret. She didn't want you to see her as a sick person; she wanted you to see her as a desirable woman."

That was the stupidest thing Aron had ever heard. Libby was a desirable woman. How else could he ever see her?

"I was the one that headed up most of the fund raisers for Libby." Aron tried to remember if he had ever heard anything about Libby or her sickness. Surely, if his brother had been that involved, he would have known something was going on. Wouldn't he? Was he so selfish? Was he so self-absorbed that he would miss something so important?

Jacob was the philanthropist, the community activist. Just this afternoon, the Little League Advisory Board had called him. There had been a break-in at the concession stand, and he was the one who had to go and make sure everything was fixed and accounted for. Who would want to break in a concession stand? A few things had been reported missing, but mostly it was just bread and ketchup. The thief was obviously not a gourmand.

"I'm sorry, Aron. I know this has thrown you for a loop. But, it was her place to tell you, not mine." Jacob watched his brother's face. If he could take away their pain he would have done it in a heartbeat. God, he wished he had that ability – to touch the ones he loved and just take away their pain. Aron. Joseph. Libby. What a miracle it would be if such a gift existed.

"She's going to be fine," Aron assured himself as well as his brother. "She's got to get well and Joseph's got to get to feeling better. We've got a wedding to plan."

At the mention of nuptials, Libby came to life.

"Let's not talk of weddings." Libby urged.

"Oh yes, we must talk of a wedding," Aron assured her.

"Aron, I'm in remission, but the leukemia I have doesn't normally stay in remission very long." Every syllable she let leave her lips shot a dagger through his heart.

"I'm going to marry you, Libby. I want to give you as many new adventures as you can handle: a husband, a home of your own, children, Fourth of July picnics, Easter Egg Hunts – the whole shebang."

"It sounds wonderful, but we just can't count on it." Her voice was so weak it scared the living daylights out of Aron.

"Jacob, write it on the calendar. We're getting married, Libby and I, three months from tonight. What day will that be?"

Jacob did some math in his head and came up with an answer. "October the 16th."

Libby smiled, "The sweetest day."

"What?" Aron was trying to follow, but he was worried sick.

"October the 16th is designated as the sweetest day." Libby's voice was weak, but she was paying attention.

"That sounds about right, Libby-mine. Any day when you became my wife would be the sweetest day that the sun ever rose to brighten the sky."

"Jacob, will you be my best man?" Aron was not leaving anything to chance. Before they reached that hospital, he wanted Libby to realize he was dead-serious about their having a future."

"There are four others who will want in on the festivities." Jacob assured Libby.

"Who do you want to ask to be your bridesmaids?" Aron asked her.

"I don't have anybody to ask." Libby confessed softly.

"That's all right," Aron reassured her. Jacob and the boys will get right on the task of finding themselves some women. We have a need for them; every beautiful bride deserves beautiful bridesmaids."

"We'll get right on it," Jacob assured them.

***

Doc Mulligan met them at the hospital. Aron didn't like the worried expression on his face. Libby made the introductions and the Doctor was glad to shake their hands.

Aron wasn't shy about identifying himself as Libby's fiancé. This pleased Doc Mulligan to no end. "Well, I have never been more honored to meet anyone in my life. Did you know we would sit and talk about you?"

Aron wondered at the doctor's comment. Libby smiled a weak little smile and told Aron, "One of the last doctor's orders I received from him was that I should go out and find someone to love."

"This is the sweetest little girl I know." It was obvious the doctor cared more about Libby that just a normal doctor/patient relationship.

"You'll get no argument from me about that." Aron shook hands with the doctor and then introduced him to his brother.

"I have to take her back now, and run a whole mess of tests." He explained to Aron. "You can pass the time out in the waiting room or leave your cell phone number and go to a hotel; I'll have one of the nurses call you when I get some answers."

With hat in hand, Aron stood his ground. "Thanks, but no thanks. I'll be just outside the door."

"So will I," Jacob chimed in.

This didn't sit well with Libby. "Why don't you go get some rest, Aron? It's late. You and Jacob are both tired."

Neither of them would budge. "I can't rest away from you, Libby-mine." He gave her a sweet, slow kiss. "I'll be right here. You hurry back to me."

The doctor took her behind closed doors and the waiting began. "What do you think they're doing to her?" Aron asked Jacob.

"Blood tests, I would think."

"Have you prayed?" Aron knew the answer, but knew Jacob would find a way to make him feel better.

"I have prayed for her every day she has been with us. I knew from the start that you two belonged together. After all you've been through, Libby and her guileless goodness was just what you needed."

"God wouldn't take her from me, would he?" Aron asked the one question that Jacob had no way to answer.

He tried anyway.

"Libby is going to be fine."

Four hours later, a nurse called his name. "Mr. McCoy?" Both he and Jacob jumped, but it was Aron who rose and followed the uniformed woman dressed all in white.

The doctor was sitting on a stool beside Libby.

Aron couldn't read his expression.

"I need to talk to the both of you. I found something."

Aron's heart flipped over. This couldn't be good. Usually, when a doctor says he has found something, it's a tumor or something worse – if that were possible.

"What is it?" Libby's face was more peaceful than

he had ever seen it. In fact, there was a glow of contentment to her countenance. Aron thought he knew why. Libby was in love. With him. And no matter what the doctor had found, no matter what the final diagnosis might be, their love would stand unchanged and eternal.

"What did you find?" Aron wondered if he would wish he had never asked the question.

"Well, I have good news." The doctor paused for effect. "The remission is still holding strong." Aron let out a huge sigh of relief. He moved across the room and grabbed his baby. She let him hold her, he could tell she was almost in shock, her whole body was trembling.

After a few moments, Aron's thinking ability began to kick back in. "What about the symptoms, her nausea and lightheadedness?"

"That wasn't all the news I had." The doctor seemed to have a flair for the dramatic.

What other news could there possibly be? Libby's remission was still holding on.

"What else, Doc?" Libby asked nervously. What if he gave her another timetable to worry about counting down?

"The nausea and sickness in question does have a source." Doc had an unreadable expression on his face.

Oh, no. What else could be wrong?

They waited for the verdict.

Throwing up his hands, Doc Mulligan nearly whooped with glee. "Libby's pregnant. She's going to have a baby!"

No one said a word. Noises from down the hall could be heard, but in their room there was nothing.

Finally, Libby broke the silence. "Pregnant?" She couldn't believe it. Putting her hands on her stomach, she moved them over the flat area in disbelief. "I'm pregnant? With a baby?"

Aron was ecstatic. He went to the bed, scooped Libby up and spun her around and around. Doc Mulligan cautioned him. "That might not be the wisest move considering her bouts of morning sickness."

Aron agreed. He slowed her to a halt, and then held her close. "I love you. I love you. I love you," he whispered.

"I never expected this," she looked at him through tear filled eyes. Doc stepped out to give them a bit of privacy and to get the papers ready for them to go.

"My prayers were answered." Aron had no doubt about that.

They held one another for a few more minutes, then Libby thought of his brother. "Jacob's waiting. Go to him."

"Okay, I'll be right back." He sat her carefully on the bed. Aron went out and told Jacob the good news, the first revelation – the remission news. He wanted to save the announcement about the baby until all the brothers could be together, including Joseph.

"Thank goodness, something is going right." Jacob sighed with relief.

He drove the couple back home. Libby slept most of the way, exhausted from the ordeal of testing. Aron held her most of the time, he was content to just watch her sleep.

"You love her don't you?" Jacob observed happily.

"More than my next breath."

"I want what you have. And as God as my witness, I'm going to find it." Jacob vowed.

***

All at Tebow Ranch was peacefully still as dawn broke. Not everything was perfect; one of their own still lay in a rehabilitation center, broken from a fall. But

182

time was righting the wrongs and smoothing out the wrinkles. The balance which had been lost years ago was finally righting itself.

Upstairs, in the master bedroom, Aron crooned to Libby. "See, everything is going to be all right." Aron looked deep into her eyes, making sure she digested every word he said.

"Yes, I believe you."

"You said I didn't have to say that I love you, but I did. My love for you is my life's truth." He stroked her hair back from her brow, tracing the beloved features of her face. "Your love defines me. It is my reason for living." Aron hadn't known he could wax poetic, but the words were flowing from him unbidden. He had to make her understand. "You are my reason for existing, Libby. I love you with a love deeper than the sea – a love that will last longer than forever."

Libby turned in his arms and held on to him for dear life. "I often doubted whether or not I would get to live. But now that I know that God has granted me grace-days, I want to put them to the best use. Aron, my love, I devote my life to living just for you."

"There will be decades of days. We're going to grow old together. You, me, our children and all of my brothers and their families – Tebow Ranch is going to be a place of love and laughter." Aron gently unbuttoned Libby's night shirt, opening it all the way so he could lay his head over his unborn child. "I can promise you both one thing, a day will never go by that I don't tell the two of you how much you mean to me. I will tell you I love you every day for the rest of my life."

***

Joseph was ready to go home. He had one of the

cute little nurses' aides get all of his gear together. Isaac and Noah would be after him and in a matter of hours he would be back on Tebow land.

If he had to live the life of a cripple, at least he could live it at home. The doctors and nurses were optimistic, but an optimistic outlook was hard for him to maintain. Was he going to have to live like this forever? Was there anyone in the world who could help him?

The soundless cry for help rose from his bed and reverberated out into the universe – and lo and behold, as the old fairy tales read – someone was listening. A connection was made. Help was on the way. Sometimes there are wonders in this world that go beyond the realm of understanding.

***

Back at the ranch, a door creaked open and a shadow slipped along the wall outside the barn. Several cows lowed in protest. There was a stranger on Tebow land. No one in the house heard anything. The stranger went to the stock tank, stripped quickly and then used the warm water to wash off the day's grime. After a few moments of stolen luxury, the small form slipped back to the barn. There was food in the small refrigerator upstairs. Maybe, no one would miss just a little. The bed was too nice to sleep in. Beggars and thieves didn't have to be totally classless. So after eating a bit of ketchup and bread, she went down to one of the stalls, curled herself down deep into the hay and settled down to sleep. Before dropping off, she made a wish: please keep me safe, please let me find a place in this world, and please let me find someone to love. She prayed her wish would come true.

***

The sun rose in a celebration of pinks and oranges as Noah pulled into the hospital parking lot. At the double electric doors, Joseph was already waiting in his wheel chair, accompanied by two doting nurses. One of them leaned over and kissed him goodbye. "Look at that," Isaac chuckled. "Hard-head don't let stuff keep him down for long." Noah wasn't as light-hearted as his brother; he could see the strain around Joseph's mouth and knew this was going to be one long, hard haul.

"About time you two got here, I've been sitting out here for a half-hour." Joseph complained. The little blonde aide shook her head at Isaac, telling him Joseph was stretching the truth quite a bit.

"The sun's just coming up, Knothead." Isaac was affectionate, but not ready to cut his brother much slack. He knew if they started babying Joseph, he might not bounce back as quickly as he would otherwise.

"How's Libby?" Joseph quietly asked as Noah helped him into the front seat of the King Ranch.

"She's home. Aron had to take her to the doctor." Isaac had spouted off the information before Noah could shush him. Even though the news was good, they didn't need to upset him anymore than he already was.

"Doctor? Libby's been to the doctor?" The concern in Joseph's voice was evident. The brother's did not know Libby had confided in Joseph before she had anyone else.

"Way to go asshole!" Noah grumbled good-naturedly at Isaac as he slung Joseph's bag into the back seat. "Libby's fine. She got a good report, but I'll let her or Aron tell you all about it. They got in late last night and went straight to bed. There's a family meeting just as soon as we can get you back to Tebow.

Joseph smiled. If Libby was all right, then maybe

the fates would have good things in store for him, also.

***

"Wake up, Beautiful." Aron sat by Libby holding a cup of coffee. Opening her eyes a tiny bit, and realizing what Aron held in his hand, she made such a ruckus Aron was afraid he was going to spill hot coffee on her. "Easy, Baby. Easy."

"God, Aron! I'm so sorry, I've overslept." Careful not to jostle him further, she turned to wiggle out on the other side. "I need to fix breakfast!" Glancing at the clock, she squealed. "Look at the time! Joseph will be here any minute!" While she was still scrambling around trying to get out from under the covers, she finally realized Aron was laughing. He was holding the blanket down on both sides of her so all of her attempts to move were fruitless.

"I've already fixed breakfast, Wiggle-worm," Aron sat the coffee on the bedside table and stretched out beside her. "Did you think I would let you get up and work after the hard day you had yesterday?" Bracketing her pillow with his arms, he leaned over to get his good morning kiss.

Libby didn't need much persuading; she gave her kiss as freely as she had given her heart. "You taste so good," she savored Aron's affection, happy in the knowledge she had a future with this glorious man.

"I've been nibbling on the pumpkin pancakes. I used your recipe."

"It's not the pancakes that taste so good to me – it's the love. I can taste love on your lips," she smiled at him with a happiness and hope in her eyes he had never seen before. "I love you, Aron," she said simply.

Aron cradled her body up close to his. "I love you. More than I'll ever be able to tell you. An ole' country boy like me just doesn't have all the pretty words that a woman like you deserves to hear."

"You're perfect and everything you do is perfect." Libby reveled in the adoration she saw in Aron's eyes.

"You're just prejudiced, the general female population doesn't view me through the same pair of rose-colored glasses that you do." He carefully traced her eyes and nose with his lips, relishing the fact that Libby was his, healthy and pregnant.

"You belong to me!" Libby's gruff little tone tickled the heck out of Aron.

"You bet your bottom dollar I do!" He had something to talk to her about, something he just had to understand. "Sweetheart, can I ask you something?" He lay flat on his back and pulled her on top of him, resting her head underneath his chin.

"Sure." Libby sighed against him. No more secrets.

"How did you end up with Freedom?" He no more had the words out that she raised up to gauge his expression.

"You found it?" Her voice was small and quiet. She didn't know why she was embarrassed; it wasn't like she had stolen it or anything.

"When I went to look for your slippers, I found it at the bottom of Bess's closet."

Playing with the buttons on his shirt, she refused to look him in the eye. "I bought it at the fair; I used my birthday money from my parents and grandparents."

"I've been looking for it for years. I made it for my Mom; it was never supposed to be sold." There was no judgment in his voice, he was just stating facts.

A stricken look passed over her face, "I'm sorry, I didn't know. I've had it all this time." Before Aron could explain, big tears started rolling down her face. "I wish I'd known; I would have given it back." She said it all so fast, and moved off of him before he could even begin to react. "Let me get it for you."

Cussing a blue streak, Aron followed her. "Wait, Libby. Do you think I care that you have it? Libby! Don't run; you'll hurt yourself!" Aron found her on the floor of the closet, cradling the bronze in her arms. He sank down beside her, berating himself for making her cry. "I love that you have it, Libby. I'm not mad."

She searched his face, trying to read between the lines. "But, you said..." She held it out to him, wordlessly returning her most treasured possession to its rightful owner. "I knew it didn't cost enough, I should never have been able to afford something so beautiful." Aron took Freedom from her and sat it down, choosing to draw her into his arms instead.

"Don't you dare cry. Everything I own is yours, including this piece of baked clay." She didn't automatically put her arms around him, and he started trying to do it for her, willing to cut off his hand before he hurt her again. "I just wanted to know why you bought it, Honey – I'm thrilled you've had it all these years. It makes the connection between us just make that much more sense. Fate was binding us together. Did you know The Rockwell Foundation was set up in memory of my mother? All of this time our lives were intertwined."

Crawling up in his lap, she poured out her heart. "I can't believe it. I confess I've wanted you for years. I went to every football game and every rodeo until I..."

"Until what?" He couldn't believe she had been his for all of these years. What damn wasted time!

"Until I got sick," He caught all of her tears, kissing them away. "When I saw that beautiful horse, he looked so wild and free, I thought if I could just have it for my own, some of its power and spirit would pass to me. And it made me feel closer to you." Bowing her head, she whispered. "Silly, wasn't it?"

"I don't think so. Look at us, we're here, we're together. And you are healthy AND pregnant. I'd say it all worked out just about perfect." He stood up and picked her up, statue and all.

"So, I can keep it?" she patted the bronze as they walked down the hall toward his room, sounding exceedingly pleased.

"Libby, everything I own belongs to you. You can have that statue and I will make you a thousand more." Thinking how he thought his world was ending just the night before, made the events of this morning heart-wrenchingly sweet.

"Just give me one when we the baby is born, how's that?" She looked at him so trustingly he thought his chest would burst with love.

"Done. I'll make you something perfect. Promise." Setting her on the bed, he put slippers on her feet. She just marveled at the wonder of having someone like him care so much for someone like her. "Your coffee is cold by now. Let's get your robe and go down and wait on the rest of the family. I bet Nathan and Jacob are down there waiting on us. Nathan has been begging to see you since we got back last night."

A horn blew outside and Libby nearly bounced out of his arms. "Joseph!" she screamed. "Let's go, Aron!" Laughing, he slung her up on his shoulder like a sack of potatoes.

"Libby!" Nathan hugged her before Aron could put her down. "Libby, are you all right?" There was so much concern in his voice that Libby almost cried.

"I'm right as rain." She hugged Nathan till he squirmed, then she went down the line and gave Jacob a hug. "Thanks for going with us last night. I don't know what we would have done without you."

"That's what brothers are for," Jacob kissed her on the end of the nose. Aron allowed it, he was too happy to be grouchy.

As soon as the door opened on the King Ranch everyone was crowded around to help Joseph out. "Hey, give me room, you bums!" Then he spotted Libby. "Not you, Libby! You come here." Joseph pulled her to him and whispered. "You went to the doctor?"

She held the sweet dare-devil close and answered, "Still cancer free." He squeezed her triumphantly.

"Somebody hand me my dang wheelchair." Aron helped his brother, wondering at the secret words which had passed between his beloved and his brother. He wasn't worried, just curious.

They assisted Joseph in and made it as far as the dining table. Aron looked around at his family. His family. Joseph had an uphill battle, but he had plenty of people ready to support him. Aron fixed an eagle eye on Joseph, "What were you and my baby whispering about?"

Everyone was filling their plates and Libby was busy pouring cold glasses of milk for all the oversize McCoy men. Joseph looked at him squarely. "Libby set me straight. Don't be mad at her, but when I was feeling sorry for myself and wondering if life was worth living as half a man – she told me the nightmare she had been facing for over half her life."

Aron felt torn. Part of him wanted to be the only one Libby confided in, but the biggest part of him was relieved she cared enough for his brother to say whatever it took to make him want to give life a chance. Aron slapped his brother on the back. "I'm glad she was there for you. Libby is something else. I'm glad you're home."

After everybody was served, Aron pulled Libby into his lap and looked at his brothers. "We have some announcements to make." Before they even began, Libby started to blush. Aron kissed the rosy glow. "It's okay."

"Are you two getting married?" Nathan's eyes shone with excitement.

"Why do you go and steal my thunder, boy?" Aron playfully cuffed his little brother. "Yes, we are. Libby is going to be a part of this family – AND –," he played it for all it was worth. "You, Mr. Nathan, are going to be an uncle."

At Aron's announcement there was a general ecstatic chaos. Libby was grabbed and passed from brother to brother, receiving kisses and hugs and congratulations. Aron was generally being ignored, but it was all right. "Hey, be gentle with the munchkin."

She was gently placed by Isaac in Joseph's lap for a final hug before she was returned to Aron. "I'm so happy for you. You've had your miracle. Now, let's work on mine."

Jessie listened to the happiness inside of the big, inviting home and wished she were part of it. Pressing her face to the glass like a child at a candy store, she watched the one they called Jacob as he quietly surveyed the celebration. He was the reason she was here. After he had almost caught her at the Little League concession stand, she had hung back and watched him work with the children. Never had she known such a man existed. He was patient and kind, working with the boys as if they were his own. But they weren't. She'd watched him leave alone. The next night when he had come, Jessie hadn't even hesitated. She had stowed away in the back of his truck, not knowing where he was going, but knowing where ever he was, that was where she wanted to be.

The pancakes smelled so good, and her stomach

growled so loudly Jessie was afraid they could hear. Most of the ketchup and bread was gone, so she was on short rations. Jessie wasn't stealing; she made sure she did work every day to pay for the food she ate. No one had noticed yet, but she was cleaning the tack and mucking the stalls. Most likely each one of the men would think one of the others was doing it. Nevertheless, it made Jessie feel better.

Taking one last look at the happy family, she sighed. Something wonderful had happened. She could tell by the smiles and the laughter. For a few minutes, she took it in. The beautiful girl was so lucky. She was loved by all six of the men, and Jessie had no one.

Sadly, she backed away and returned to the barn. Now, would be a good time to take a dip in the stock tank. Everyone was safely occupied and there would be no chance she would get caught. Carefully, she opened the barn door. The cows and horses were used to her now. She had made sure to pet each one and even slipped them some of the nuggets which were stored in the feed bin. Now, they looked at her expectantly, but none set off any type of alarm. She had claimed the last stall on the right next to the big Palomino. Speaking to the golden horse, she shed her clothes and folded them neatly in the corner. Only having two sets made her keep everything neat. "Thanks for the use of your blanket, Gorgeous." She spoke to the horse; he looked exactly as if he understood every word. Wrapping the horse blanket around her, Jessie stole away to bathe.

***

Nathan was so relieved Libby and Aron had gotten together. He may only be thirteen, but he knew the ropes. He could see it coming a mile away. And now, Libby was pregnant. There was going to be an actual, small human being coming to live on Tebow. For the first time, he wouldn't be the baby. So, it was high time they quit treating him like one. Like now. Noah had lost his cell-phone out of his truck and he had been given the thankless job of backtracking all over the place to hunt it. Making his way to the corral, Nathan passed close to the stock tank. Hearing a splash, he almost jumped out of his skin. Slipping around, Nathan was determined to catch the intruder. Easing close, he stood on tip-toe and what he saw made him gasp.

To a thirteen year old, long hair and glistening water on a near naked female could only mean one thing. Turning to run, he began to holler. "Guys, guys! Come quick!" Of course, no one could hear him, except Jessie, who quickly scrambled to get out of the tank. Racing back to the house, he threw open the kitchen door and found Jacob in the midst of kitchen duty.

"Hey, what's wrong with you? You know you're not supposed to slam the door, and look at the mud you're tracking in on Libby's clean floor." Nathan was panting, and more excited than Jacob could remember seeing him.

"Jacob, come quick!" He tried to pull his brother to the door.

"Why? Is the barn on fire?" Jacob knew how boys could flip out over the least little thing.

"No, you've gotta come see." Nathan was insistent.

"See what buddy?" Nathan's enthusiasm was contagious.

"You just won't believe it." At Jacob's stern expression, Nathan held open the door and motioned his brother to follow him with a pleading look on his face. "You've got to see this, Jacob. It's better than the time Isaac found that two-headed snake."

"If you don't just spit it out, I'm going to ground

you from your Wii."

Nathan wasn't worried – he knew Jacob's bark was worse than his bite. "For God's sake, Jacob. I've been trying to tell you! There's a mermaid in the stock tank!"

"Well, you're right." Jacob followed his brother out the door. "This I've got to see."

**

Libby's pancakes hadn't set well with her at all. Aron bathed her face and handed her some crackers and coke. She had been sick again, but this time there had been relief and joy in the nausea. For now she knew the sickness stemmed from her pregnancy and not from a relapse into leukemia. "All better?" Aron lifted her chin so he could see her expression clearly.

"Yes, all better," she nodded. "I'm just so tired."

"Why don't you lie down and rest for a while? We've had way too much excitement in the last few days." She wasn't hard to convince, and soon he had her nestled down in the soft covers. "I should be out fixing fences, but I can't seem to drag myself away from you," Aron stroked her face. "I love you, Libby.

She smiled at him, then said something which made his mouth fall open. "You don't have to say you love me, Aron."

Confused, he asked, "We've talked about this, you know I do. Don't you like to hear me say I love you?"

Snuggling up to him, she explained. "Oh, I love to hear about your love for me." Pulling his shirt out of his pants and then proceeding to undo his belt buckle, she went on to clarify her surprising statement. "But you don't have to say it out loud. You say it so clearly in so many other ways." One of those ways was poking up through his underwear.

"What do you mean?" He was fast losing his ability

to verbally communicate. His attention and oxygen giving blood supply was all headed south.

"Your eyes tell me you love me." She kissed his eyelids softly. "Your hands tell me you love me." Libby picked up each hand and caressed the palm with her lips. "Your body tells me you love me," she got his total attention when her small hands closed around his stone-hard cock. "But most of all, it's a heart to heart communication." She pressed her breasts to his chest so they could feel one another's quickly elevating heartbeat.

Aron was tearing off his clothes, and then he started on hers. "Non-verbal communication can be very effective." Spreading her legs, he readied her to receive him. "You are so hot, Libby. Your heat burns me alive." Kissing a path down her body, Aron showed Libby how much he cared. "Every day, Liberty Bell, I will make sure you know that I love you – in every way I'm able."

And he was very Able.

Ready. Willing. And definitely Able.

Read on for more from

Sable Hunter

Hot on Her Trail
(Hell Yeah!)

http://myBook.to/HotOnHerTrail

Stepping into the small opening that was naturally formed by a circle of very tall golden sunflowers, he saw her sitting there looking like a wood nymph. Her hair was windblown and her cheeks were like little red apples that had been kissed by the sun. Blue was too tame a word for her eyes. They were dancing as bright as moonlight on the water. "This was where my dad proposed to my mom. At that time, it was just the well sitting out in a field of wildflowers. There's an old legend in our family that if a woman looks down into this old well and makes a wish, she'll see the face of the person she's supposed to marry." Jacob squatted down in front of her, enjoying the view. Did she realize why he was telling her all of this? "Mom swore on a stack of Bibles she saw Dad's face. This old well became their spot. When he proposed, he did it here. And when they got married, Dad planted this huge field of sunflowers for her because they were her favorite. He replanted it every year, making it bigger and bigger until you have the twelve acres it is now."

Struck by the magic of the story, Jessie hopped up and walked to the well, trying with all of her might to push the concrete covering to one side. Smiling with indulgence, Jacob stepped up behind her and added his muscle until the cover moved easily. "Look down in there, Jess. Tell me what you see."

Jessie stood on her tiptoes and put her forearms on the lip of the well, gazing down into the waters. She could see the waning blue of the sky reflected into the clear pool, as well as a ring of colorful sunflowers. Her own face peered back. "I see me." She laughed. Looking over her shoulder at Jacob, she wrinkled her nose at him and smiled. "Either, it has to be dark or I'm doomed to be an old maid." Jacob moved in closer, blanketing her back with his wide, warm chest.

"Look again, Precious."

Heart pounding in her chest, Jessie gazed back down into the dark waters alive with the reflections of their world. Jacob's face was reflected next to hers, but he wasn't looking at the water. He was looking at her with the most intense look of love she had ever seen. Jessie gasped! Surely, it was an illusion.

"Who do you see, Jess?"

Mercy! Jessie fought every instinct that told her to run, to get away, because what she was seeing couldn't be real. It must be a trick of the light. Deciding to preserve her dignity, Jessie made light of the intense moment. "I see a handsome cowboy." Pretending she was looking closer, she said. "I think its Matt Damon!" she said in a kidding tone.

"Why you, little..." Jacob grabbed Jessie, picked her up, and blew on her belly. "Would you rather have Matt Damon than me?" He nipped at her playfully. She was giggling so hard, she was about to lose her breath.

At his question, Jessie sobered. It was unacceptable for him to think she would ever desire anyone more than she did him. "No, no," Jessie ran her hand through his thick dark hair. "I want no one, but you. Only you."

Wolf Call

http://myBook.to/WolfCall

Rafe took one step toward her. She held her ground. Brave woman. The corner of his lip lifted in a crooked, wicked smile. Another step. The music playing in the background had a seductive beat, a soundtrack of lust. Her eyes were glued to his, Rafe could hear her breathing from where she stood. His hearing was acute and selective. He sniffed the air again, she was aroused. Good. The urge to shift almost overwhelmed him, never had he been tempted in a public place. His mind battled with his instinct and he stamped it down. One more step and he held out his hand. "Dance?"

Karoline's whole body tingled. Who was this guy? Sex on a stick, definitely. She'd seen good-looking men before, but her body had never lit up like it was doing now. Her breasts were throbbing, her sex was aching and she found herself moving toward him. When their fingers touched, she shook. It was like connecting two sources of high voltage. And when he pulled her body next to his, she trembled in his arms. "I wasn't planning on dancing, I just wanted to watch. I don't have very good rhythm." He stared into her eyes and Karoline found it hard to breathe.

"Just follow my lead. I'll set the pace." The magnetic man tightened his grip around her waist and traced the line of her cheek. "Your skin is baby soft, so tender. I bet you're amazing to touch."

He said the last word in a whisper that brushed over her neck. Karoline's sex clenched in absolute surrender. Even she knew he was talking about touching her in secret, exciting places. "You come on strong."

Rafe rubbed his nose in her hair. "Subtlety has never been my strong suit."

Dancing close to him, song after song, Karoline's mind was in a whirl. He flirted, he charmed, he stole gentle touches specifically designed to draw her under his spell. She'd only come to the bar because she had some time to kill. The lodge where she had reservations wasn't available till the morning. Being swept off her feet by a man such as this was a fantasy of hers, but not one she expected to come to life. "I wasn't prepared for you. You're making me dizzy."

He was fully aroused and there was no way she could miss it, he was rubbing his cock against her belly with every step. "I know what I want when I see it."

"And what would that be?" Her voice was weak, she realized that. This man was like no one she'd ever encountered. Being around him was heady, he made her quiver with need. Karoline had only been with one other man in her life and that milksop hadn't prepared her for this beast.

"You."

Karoline swallowed. Had she lost her mind? Maybe too much time alone in the wilderness had robbed her of civilized behavior, but she found herself responding wholeheartedly to this self-assured god with the hard, buff body. "Don't I get a drink first?"

"I'll get a bottle of champagne to go. My place or yours?" Rafe was on fire. If he didn't get inside this woman soon, he'd explode.

Okay, at least she could be a tad wise. "Mine. You're not married or otherwise committed, are you? I don't do that." She didn't do anything, really. Karoline Durand was a loner. Her occupation necessitated it.

"Footloose and fancy free," Rafe mumbled. "My taxes are paid, I'm a Southern gentleman and I go to church on Sundays. You?"

"Same, I'm single. But I haven't been to church in years." She laid her head on his shoulder and groaned at how good her breasts felt mashed up against his hard chest.

Laughter rumbled in his chest. "I won't hold that against you."

"Good thing, what you're holding against me is more than I can handle." She blushed as she said the bold words.

"Oh, I bet you can handle me. Don't you want to try?"

A WISHING MOON

http://myBook.to/AWishingMoon

She cut short her self-pampering and instead of the revealing teddy she had bought in town today, she put on a much more sensible long gown and robe. Arabella had no idea the black negligee was much sexier than the blatant red set she'd been tempted to wear.

Slipping down the stairs, she hoped she did not run into anybody between her room and Jade's. She didn't think she could stand any comments from her mother about her choice of sleeping attire. Another thing she felt thankful for was the location of the room they would be sleeping in. Thankfully, they were on a different floor and at opposite ends of the house from where the rest of the family slept.

She hesitated at the door. Her nerves were on edge and her body was tingling, readying itself for his possession. Already, her breasts were swelling and both nipples were as hard as rocks. She couldn't wait to be in his arms again. Taking the doorknob in her hand, she held it for a moment and then slowly opened the door. When she entered the room, Jade waited, already in the bed. Leaning back against the headboard, propped up by two or three soft pillows, he looked like a dream. With no shirt on, the soft light of the lamp accentuated his broad shoulders and golden skin. After finding out he had a Cherokee grandparent, the color and smoothness of his skin made sense. He held the covers back and patted the mattress in invitation.

Crossing to the bed, she removed her robe and swiftly crawled under the covers. He eased down in the bed and turned on his side and facing her. "You are so beautiful, Arabella."

She lowered her eyes, unable to breathe if she continued to share his gaze. His eyes were looking into her very soul. "No, you are beautiful, Jade. I have never known anyone who makes me feel the way you do."

"How many men am I competing with, sweetheart?" he asked in a soft, gentle tone.

"What do you mean?"

"How many men are you dating? I'm sure there is a whole slew of them just beating your door down, all wanting the privilege of your company."

"There is no one." Now that the truth would be revealed, he probably wouldn't be as interested in her.

"No one?"

"I'm sorry, Jade. I don't have very much experience with men." Her voice shook slightly and she closed her eyes waiting for his reaction. How could she tell him the local boys had all been afraid of her, or at least afraid of the ridicule they would endure by dating the town witch?

Light, soft, sweet kisses began raining on her eyes and her cheeks. "Why are you sorry, Bella? Don't you know how exciting it is for a man to find out his woman hasn't known many other men?"

"Not exactly what I meant," Arabella stammered. God, this was hard.

"Quit worrying, Arabella," Jade assured her. "The other men are history. You're here with me now."

"No, Jade." She grabbed the hand caressing her neck and lightly playing over the top of her full breasts. He wasn't making this easy. "The only man I have ever made love to is you—in our dreams." She waited for his reaction. What if he didn't want a twenty-four year-old virgin?

A BREATH OF HEAVEN

http://myBook.to/ABreathofHeaven

Abby noticed Cade and Jase exchanging a knowing look. Jase slapped his best friend on the shoulder. "Be careful. I have to warn you, she's armed."

Cade snorted. "Your sister is always armed. She's lethal. But I do enjoy a challenge. Taming flighty, feisty fillies is my specialty."

Jase put on his coat, easing out into the inclement weather as Abby grumbled. Cade ducked and a rosy red apple bounced off the door. "Tame me?" She picked up another apple and considered her target. "You don't have the balls, Tallbull." Even as she threw down the gauntlet, Abby knew she'd just made a strategic mistake. She'd just waved a red cape in the face of the biggest bull Alpha in Texas. Damn! Why did he have to be so devastatingly good-looking? Every time she was near him, her whole body went into sexual shell-shock. Six-foot three, two-hundred forty pounds, perfectly ripped, wide shoulders, coal black eyes, dark hair and enough scruff to make him look like an old west desperado. Yea, he was gorgeous and she wanted to run for the hills.

Cade began to move toward her. Slowly.

Abby was no fool. She started backing up.

"Au contraire, my lady." Cade cupped his oversize package in the palm of his hand and bucked his hips toward her slightly. Abby jumped. "Do I make you

204

nervous, Buttercup?" Cade wanted to lick the fluttering pulse point at the base of her neck so badly he could taste it. "I'm hung, Abby. Don't ever doubt it. You wanna see? I'll be glad to show you. I have a yard of hard, a battleship full of balls and enough hair—"

"For heaven sakes, stop it!" Abby couldn't take anymore. Before she knew it, he had her backed against the wall - literally. "You Are Out Of Line, Cade," she growled out every word.

Placing one big hand on either side of her head, Cade leaned over and looked her right in the eye. She could feel his breath on her face. She could smell him – God, he smelled good. A scant quarter of an inch separated their bodies. Her breasts were swelling. Abby dared not breathe, lest the hungry tips graze his chest.

Lowering his voice, Cade whispered in her ear. "A moment ago, when you thrust your shoulders back, did you know it made me want to suck your nipples?"

Her sex wept at his words, clenching with need. "Jerk!" She pushed against his chest, lightly, but he didn't budge. Abby wasn't nearly as brave or disinterested as she pretended.

Cade licked his lips and winked at her. "I bet I could make you tremble, Abilene. Do you remember that one sweet kiss we shared all those years ago? You sure enjoyed it. I can still remember how you whimpered and clung to me, pressing those sweet tits of yours into my chest."

Abby stiffened, the memory almost hurt more than she could bear. "The kiss was a mistake, a terrible mistake." He could never know the truth—never.

Still bracketing Abby's body, he let his eyes rove over her face, trying to read her emotions. "No, you're wrong. The kiss was amazing," he countered. Cade let his mask of teasing drop. Sighing, he looked almost sad for a moment. "I've never understood what happened to change your mind or why just being around me gets your panties in such a twist." Then, he grinned again – picking up where he left off. His demeanor changed, Cade lost the wistful expression and gave her an evil little smirk. "But let me put your mind at ease, Shortcake. As far as I'm concerned, spending time with you is like going to the dentist. A necessary evil. Because rest assured, I want to be here with you about as much as you want me here."

A burning slash of pain almost split Abby in two. Cade's words stung like a fiery brand was thrust in her side. If he only knew the truth…

"Fine." She grated, pushing on his chest once more. His hard, muscled, manly chest. "I understand you completely and I agree. Just stay out of my way while you're here. Now, move!" She pushed again—hard— and he smoothly stepped to one side.

Her momentum caused Abby to gallop out into the middle of the floor, much to Cade's amusement.

"Steady, Abs, you're gonna fall on that delectable tush."

Cade chuckled. Abby fumed. "Let me show you to your room. And I hope you stay in there!" She ground out her words. "Follow me, Tallbull."

"To the ends of the earth, Darlin'."

His sexy drawl just made her even more furious. The man was stepping on her very last nerve – and he knew it. "Yea, right."

He grabbed his bags and she led the way. There was only one guest room and now she wished it was on the far side of the house instead of right next door to hers.

UNCHAINED MELODY

http://myBook.to/UnchainedMelody

"What ifs will drive us crazy, Ethan." His hand came up and rubbed her knee in slow, soft circles. She got up and walked away, needing to put distance between them.

Desperate, thinking quickly, he decided to try another tactic.

"Will you go out to dinner with me tomorrow? Just dinner—that's all I ask."

"I don't know, Ethan." What would it accomplish—just more torture for her.

He might be sorry, but he just had to know. "Have I changed, Lise? Do you still find me sexually attractive? Don't you want me anymore?"

She couldn't believe the question. "What?" He must be kidding. The problem wasn't with him it lay with her. "Ethan, you are much more handsome now than you were before and you were delectable then."

Delectable, huh? That had to be good. He continued to push the envelope. "But are you physically attracted to me, now, tonight?"

Annalise bowed her head and shut her eyes. She stood up and walked to the back door of the kitchen. She knew that a path from the door led directly to her cabin. He stood up to follow her. She pointed one small finger at him. "Stay right where you are. I will answer you, but you must promise me something." He didn't answer her. "Promise!" she demanded.

"Okay, anything." He had to know.

"I will answer you and then I am walking out of here—you cannot follow me. I have to be by myself for just a little while. My emotions are in complete tatters. I need to think. Do you promise?" Her face was flushed, her breathing erratic.

He thought she was the most beautiful thing God had ever created. "I will promise not to follow you, if you will promise to have dinner with me tomorrow." He was beginning to enjoy this.

She conceded, exasperated. "All right, I will have dinner with you."

"So, answer me. Are you physically attracted to me? Do you remember what it was like making love with me? Do you still want me, Lise?"

A look of anguish came over her face that totally threw him for a loop. But her answer was music to his ears. "Yes, I find you more attractive than any man I have ever met. I remember every detail of every time we made love. I have relived it in my mind and in my fantasies, every facet of the incredible hours we shared, over and over again. And yes, I want you so much it hurts. I ache for you. I am starved for you, but—that's where it must end. I don't intend—I cannot allow myself to do anything about it." With that amazing revelation, she was gone.

Ethan was smiling. "Well, we'll just see about that, won't we?"

LOVE'S MAGIC SPELL

http://myBook.to/LovesMagicSpell

Raising her hand, she started to knock.

How would he act? She didn't want him to be a zombie while they made love. Hattie had told her he wouldn't remember tomorrow. But how would he act tonight?

"Arg!" she squealed and stomped her foot.

The door opened. Raylan stood there in nothing but his jeans and they were undone, he was wet from a shower with a towel slung over his shoulder. "Why are you on my front porch doing pirate imitations?"

Well, that answered one question, he was going to act normally.

"Can I come in?"

Raylan stood back so the love of his life could enter. This wasn't good. He was tired, horny and his resistance was almost nonexistent where she was concerned on a good day, not a day when he craved to have someone in his bed that he adored and who cared more about him than the rest of the world put together. "Be my guest." Said the spider to the fly. "What can I help you with?"

Remembering she could see through the window, she went to his blinds and shut them.

"Tory, what are you doing? Are you about to tell me some state secret or something?"

"No." She gripped the belt of her coat. "I'm not here to tell you anything. I'm here to show you something."

"What? Did someone send in new evidence?"

Closing her eyes, she went for it. "No, I'm here to

seduce you. I want you, Raylan West, and I intend to have you. Resistance is futile." With that, she opened her coat and let it fall.

Two things happened simultaneously. Rafe lost the ability to speak and his cock went rock hard. He just stood there staring. And staring. Tory had a beautiful, perfect face. And many times he'd fantasized about what she looked like beneath those cute little clothes she wore. She dressed classy, not real conservative but not overly sexy. He knew she had a good body, he could see all the curves in all the right places. But nothing—nothing—had prepared him for the wet dream standing before him. An hour glass figure with a tiny waist, luscious tits and a saucy little bottom he could barely keep his hands off of. And God, her legs…they were shapely, long and he ached to kiss her from head to toe.

OMG, is this a disaster, Tory thought. He was struck dumb, frozen, like sailors of old when they saw Medusa, the ugly woman with snakes for hair. Picking her coat up, she slung it over her shoulders. "This was a mistake."

"Don't move, don't you dare put that coat back on." Raylan took two steps and he was at her side, taking the coat from her hand and flinging it across the room. "Are you real? Are you a dream? I must've fallen and hit my head in the shower."

She didn't get a chance to answer. With one powerful pull, he had her up close and personal, flush against his body. She could feel his arousal nestled between them. "Give me that mouth," he demanded and she raised her head, marveling at the strength of the spell she had cast.

"You do want me, don't you?"

"More than you'll ever know," he whispered as he claimed her lips. The passion was riding too high. This was no kiss, this was a melding, a mating, a devouring.

210

He crushed her to him and made love to her mouth, drinking from her lips greedily, hungrily. Never still, he traced their shape with his tongue, nibbled on her upper lip and dipped his tongue inside. He drew hers to him, taking it within his mouth and sucking on it.

Tory's knees gave way and he caught her up, one hand on her waist and the other cupping the round, firm ass he planned on memorizing with fingers and kisses.

She tried to remain coherent, after all she had a plan, but he was masterful, dominating, passionate and all of that extreme maleness was focused right on her. Tory felt like a delicate piece of nothing flaring up after being kissed by the rays of the sun.

"I can't believe you came. Do you know how many nights I've dreamed of you doing this?" He was kissing her neck, his hands running over her skin.

Tory was trying to form thoughts. This spell was more powerful than she'd imagined. It had given him false memories of desiring her. Oh well, at least she could speak truth. After all, he wouldn't remember it in the morning. "I've dreamed about you too. I lie over there in my lonely bed every night and ache for you. Tonight, I just couldn't stay away."

Sable Hunter

About the Author:

Sable Hunter writes romance, some of it quite spicy. She writes what she likes to read and enjoys putting her fantasies on paper. Her stories are emotional reads where the heroine is faced with challenges, like one of her favorite songs – she's holding out for a hero – and boy, can she deliver a hero. Her aim is to write a story that will make you laugh, cry and sweat. If she can wring those emotions out of a reader, then she has done her job.

She grew up in south Louisiana along the mysterious bayous where the Spanish moss hangs thickly over the dark waters. The culture of Louisiana has shaped her outlook on life and made its way into her novels where the supernatural is entirely normal. Presently, Sable lives in Texas and spends most of her time in wild and wonderful Austin. She is passionate about animals and has been known to charm creatures from a one ton bull to a family of raccoons. For fun, Sable has been known to haunt cemeteries and battlefields armed with night-vision cameras and digital recorders hunting proof that love survives beyond the grave.

Join her in her world of magic, alpha heroes, sexy cowboys and hot, steamy, to-die-for sex. Step into the shoes of her heroines and escape to places where dreams can come true and orgasms only come in multiples.

Visit Sable:

Website: http://www.sablehunter.com

Facebook:

https://www.facebook.com/authorsablehunter

Amazon: http://www.amazon.com/author/sablehunter

Pinterest   https://www.pinterest.com/AuthorSableH/

Twitter https://twitter.com/huntersable

Sign up for Sable Hunter's newsletter

http://eepurl.com/qRvyn

SABLE'S BOOKS
Get hot and bothered!!!

Hell Yeah!

Cowboy Heat
(Hell Yeah! Book 1)
myBook.to/cowboyheat

Hot on Her Trail
(Hell Yeah! Book 2)
myBook.to/HotOnHerTrail

Her Magic Touch
(Hell Yeah! Book 3)
myBook.to/HerMagicTouch

Brown Eyed Handsome Man
(Hell Yeah! Book 4)
myBook.to/BrownEyedHandsome

Badass
(Hell Yeah! Book 5)
myBook.to/BadassHellYeah

Burning Love
(Hell Yeah! Book 6)
myBook.to/BurningLove

Forget Me Never
(Hell Yeah! Book 7)
myBook.to/ForgetMeNever

I'll See You In My Dreams

(Hell Yeah! Book 8)
myBook.to/IllSeeYouInMyDreamsHellYeah

Finding Dandi
(Hell Yeah! Book 9)
myBook.to/FindingDandiHellYeah

Skye Blue
(Hell Yeah! Book 10)
myBook.to/SkyeBlue

I'll Remember You
(Hell Yeah! Book 11)
myBook.to/IllRememberYou

True Love's Fire
(Hell Yeah! Book 12)
myBook.to/TrueLovesFire

Thunderbird
(Hell Yeah! Book 13)
myBook.to/Thunderbird-Equalizers

Welcome To My World
(Hell Yeah! Book 14)
myBook.to/WelcomeToMyWorld

How to Rope a McCoy
(Hell Yeah!)
myBook.to/ToRopeAMcCoy

One Man's Treasure
(Hell Yeah! - Equalizers)
myBook.to/OneMansTreasure

You Are Always on My Mind
(Hell Yeah! Cajun Style)
myBook.to/AlwaysOnMyMind

Hell Yeah! Sweeter Versions

Cowboy Heat - Sweeter Version
(Hell Yeah! Sweeter Version Book 1)
myBook.to/SweetCowboyHeat

Hot on Her Trail - Sweeter Version
(Hell Yeah! Sweeter Version Book2)
myBook.to/SweetHotonHerTrail

Her Magic Touch - Sweeter Version
(Hell Yeah! Sweeter Version Book 3)
myBook.to/SweetHerMagicTouch

Brown Eyed Handsome Man - Sweeter Version
(Hell Yeah! Sweeter Version Book 4)
myBook.to/SweetBrownEyedHandsomeMan

Badass - Sweeter Version
(Hell Yeah! Sweeter Version Book 5)
myBook.to/SweetBADASS

Burning Love - Sweeter Version
(Hell Yeah! Sweeter Version Book 6)
myBook.to/SweetBurningLove

Finding Dandi - Sweeter Version
 (Hell Yeah! Cajun Style)
myBook.to/SweetFindingDandi

Forget Me Never - Sweeter Version
(Hell Yeah! Book 7)
myBook.to/SweetForgetMeNever

I'll See You In My Dreams –

Sweeter Version (Hell Yeah! Book 8)
myBook.to/SweetIllSeeYouInMyDreams

Moon Magic Series
A Wishing Moon (Moon Magic Book 1)
 myBook.to/AWishingMoon

Sweet Evangeline (Moon Magic Book 2)
 myBook.to/SweetEvangeline

Hill Country Heart Series
Unchained Melody (Hill Country Heart Book 1)
 myBook.to/UnchainedMelody

Scarlet Fever (Hill Country Heart Book 2)
 myBook.to/scarletfever

Bobby Does Dallas (Hill Country Heart 3)
http://amzn.to/1LOnpff

Dixie Dreaming
Come With Me (Dixie Dreaming Book 1)
 myBook.to/ComeWithMe

Pretty Face: A Red Hot Cajun Nights Story
 myBook.to/PrettyFace

Texas Heat Series
T-R-O-U-B-L-E (Texas Heat Book 1)
 myBook.to/T-R-O-U-B-L-E

My Aliyah (Texas Heat Book 2)
 myBook.to/MyAliyah

El Camino Real Series

A Breath of Heaven (El Camino Real Book1)
  myBook.to/ABreathofHeaven

Loving Justice (El Camino Real Book 2)
 myBook.to/LovingJustic

Texas Heroes Series
Texas Wildfire   myBook.to/TexasWildfire
Texas CHAOS   myBook.to/TexasCHAOS

More From Sable Hunter:

For A Hero
myBook.to/ForAHero

Green With Envy (It's Just Sex Book 1)
myBook.to/GreenWithEnvy

Hell Yeah! Box Set With Bonus Cookbook
myBook.to/HellYeahSet

Love's Magic Spell: A Red Hot Treats Story
myBook.to/LovesMagicSpell

Wolf Call
myBook.to/WolfCall

Cowboy 12 Pack: Twelve-Novel Boxed Set
myBook.to/Cowboy12Pack

Rogue (The Sons of Dusty Walker)
myBook.to/Rogue

Be My Love Song
myBook.to/BeMyLoveSong

Audio
Cowboy Heat - Sweeter Version: Hell Yeah! Sweeter
Version
myBook.to/CowboyHeatSweetAudio

Hot on Her Trail - Sweeter Version: Hell Yeah!
Sweeter Version, Book 2
myBook.to/HOHTSweetAudio

<u>Spanish Edition</u>
Vaquero Ardiente *(*Cowboy Heat)
Amazon US http://amzn.to/1qHMi2G

Su Rastro Caliente (Hot On Her Trail)
Amazon US http://amzn.to/1u2Dd3T

Made in the USA
Thornton, CO
02/06/23 12:54:46

555573e7-0f16-44a6-a082-231ceef9463dR02